When the warrior King
castle with his train of n
lovely and impulsive as
whelmed by William's p
de Boveney, one of his

Though he and his brother Gilbert look almost identical, Alyce cannot understand how anyone could confuse two such different men. Certainly the coldly aloof Gilbert has saved her from the brutal lust of a neighbouring Count, but it is Roger who swears he loves her and gets the King's consent to marry her. And having accepted him, why should Alyce still doubt which brother has won her heart?

Lady of Starlight

Margot Holland

MILLS & BOON LIMITED
London · Sydney · Toronto

*First published in Great Britain 1981
by Mills & Boon Limited, 15–16 Brook's Mews,
London W1*

© Margot Holland 1981
This edition 1981
*Australian copyright 1981
Philippine copyright 1981*

ISBN 0 263 73434 X

The text of this publication or any part thereof may not be reproduced or transmitted in any form or by any means, electronic or mechanical, including photocopying, recording, storage in an information retrieval system, or otherwise, without the written permission of the publisher.

This book is sold subject to the condition that it shall not, by way of trade or otherwise, be lent, resold, hired out or otherwise circulated without the prior consent of the publisher in any form of binding or cover other than that in which it is published and without a similar condition including this condition being imposed on the subsequent purchaser.

Set in VIP Baskerville 10 on 11½pt by
Fakenham Press Limited

*Made and printed in Great Britain by
Cox & Wyman Ltd., Reading*

CHAPTER ONE

It had been a good day. The early showers had died away. Silver droplets still glinted on upturned leaf and petal, and the aroma of herbs, the tang of the sea, were mixed with the scent of drying earth.

A voice behind spoke in protest. 'Lady Alyce! If you've looked from that turret window once, you've looked a dozen times this day. The gate will send you word of their sighting, never fear.'

'I know, I know!' Alyce exclaimed, turning. 'But how can you go on so calmly when it is the King who comes? The King, Edith! Just imagine. Here, in the castle.'

Her old servant regarded her fondly. ' 'Tis an honour for you and your father, no doubt, but only extra work for those that must prepare the quarters for I don't know how many. The kitchen's been like the anteroom of hell since before dawn.'

'Will there be enough?' Alyce asked anxiously.

'Don't fret, my lady. There's an oxen on the spit, a fine young boar, ducks and leverets too many to count, and enough ale and baked bread to feed an army. But my lord Earl, your father, reckoned about two dozen as this is a private visit.'

Alyce nodded, then stiffened. Her head turned, listening. 'Did you hear anything, Edith?'

She flew back to the window and peered out. From this height one could see across the bailey and over the gate-towers towards the heath with the Sussex hills rising beyond. To one side was the river, running beside the woodland, to the other the land sloped roughly over wind-whipped dunes to the sea. As she scanned the countryside a flight of birds rose from the tall branches and swooped crying across the heath.

'They don't rise without reason,' she murmured, and narrowed her eyes, watching the dip between the violet hills. It was the only track from the west that could be used by a body of men and wagons. The late afternoon sun broke through the lowering clouds, ribbons of sunlight streamed down, turning the violet shadows into the greens and golds of gorseland. And like a multi-coloured flower opening its petals, she saw the knights' pennons unfurl in the breeze, blue and yellow, black and green. But her gaze searched amongst the gonfalons of the barons to find the one above all.

There it was, held aloft by the standard-bearer. The blood-red silk rippled, setting the device of two gold lions dancing. She heaved a sigh of pure bliss. King William the First, under the royal arms of England, was approaching. She would meet the King, this man her father had served under and fought with, the one they used to call the Wolf of Normandy. He was no longer young but still ruled with an iron hand. Fair and just, her father said, but merciless to those who opposed him.

They were crossing the heath now and the gonfalon of her father, Earl Robert, fluttered beside that of the King as they rode abreast. Behind them streamed the lesser barons and knights followed by squires and grooms, spare horses and baggage wagons. Two dozen nobles maybe, Alyce surmised, but an equal number of attendants to be housed and fed. At this moment she wished more than ever that her mother was still alive and might greet the guests in the great hall. But the duty was hers now, and at sixteen she was old enough to take her place.

She spun away from the window. 'Edith, my veil! I cannot receive the King uncovered.' She fled to her chamber, holding up her long white tunic with the embroidered border while Edith panted behind her.

'They'll not be here yet awhile, my lady,' she grumbled. 'Come, let me tie your hair in a knot before you put on the veil. Don't fidget so, child.' She gathered the heavy black hair and coiled it dexterously at the nape of Alyce's neck. 'Now the veil and headband.'

The filmy material fell to Alyce's waist at the back while the front was short and frilled to frame her face and held in position by an embroidered headband. Alyce reached for her gold girdle and tied it round her slender waist. The tasseled ends reached almost to the ground. The girdle was important. It could be of gold or silver cord or again of knotted coloured wool, but the material of it denoted the rank of the wearer. As an Earl's daughter, Alyce de Beaumont wore the gold cord.

She surveyed herself in the polished silver hand-mirror. Her cheeks were flushed and her brown eyes under dark brows were wide with the excitement of this visit. Her only regret was that lack of height denied her the air of maturity she so desired.

The hollow sound of hooves on the wooden drawbridge made her catch her breath.

'They're here, Edith!'

'Yes, my lady, and you should be in the hall waiting to greet His Majesty.' She smiled and curtsied. 'Be calm, my little one. 'Twill be a common duty hereafter.'

Alyce made her way down the winding steps of the only staircase in the large square-built castle. All the rooms had access to it so as not to weaken the walls with more than one stairway. Reaching the main hall she stationed herself beneath the carved archway. Behind her the trestles were set with cloths and silver plate. Shafts of sunlight sparkled on the goblets and water-jugs, casting lengthening shadows across the fine linen cloth.

Her heart beat in anticipation as heavy footsteps crossed the outer hall. The doors stood wide and she watched as light armour and glittering swords were handed to the squires. Then the room seemed full of colour and noise. She saw her father, tall, slightly stooping, head inclined deferentially, then her whole attention was riveted on the man by his side.

Of medium height and strongly built, though running to corpulence, his very presence spoke of power. The eyes held a keen intelligence. He had needed all his cunning to survive and conquer both Normandy and England; from base-born infant to the most powerful king in all Christendom was no mean feat. His father, it was true, had been of noble birth but William was born of the Duke's mistress, Arletta, a tanner's daughter. Although richly dressed, his tunic and cross-gartered hose proclaimed the soldier he would always be.

Her father was speaking and the King's grey eyes held a smile as she was presented. Sinking into a deep curtsy, she stammered, 'I bid you welcome, Your Majesty. We are honoured by your presence.'

Iron fingers reached out and lifted her and she looked into the strongly marked face. He had ruled a turbulent country for near on twenty years and was now in his late fifties, but the sharp, hawk-like look remained, and it was a brave man who rose against this born warrior.

'My Lady Alyce,' he said, 'the honour is mine. I knew your mother, God rest her soul, and you bid to become as fair a lady. Allow me to present my young knights who are eager for your acknowledgement.'

Alyce became aware of the men grouped about the King. She smiled and curtsied, missing their names completely as her gaze widened and fell upon two seemingly identical knights.

William laughed. 'These are the brothers de Boveney, mistress. The elder by one year is Gilbert and the younger is

Roger. 'Tis difficult to tell them apart on first acquaintance, and yet the difference will soon become apparent to you.' He fell into talk with Earl Robert and she was left facing the brothers. The other knights paled into insignificance beside these two.

Both men bowed and smiled, but in the smile of the one called Roger there seemed to lurk a merriment that attracted her instantly. She gauged them as being, perhaps, in their early twenties.

'I trust you will be well entertained, gentlemen,' she said formally. 'There are hawks in the mews and a bear-hunt is arranged for your pleasure on the morrow. Even a tournament a day later for the King's diversion.'

'And with your gracious presence, my lady, we could not ask more,' said Sir Roger, his eyes warm and flattering. 'What do you say, Gil?'

'What?' Sir Gilbert turned from his survey of the hall. Alyce went hot with anger. He had not even listened to her words of welcome! He even looked bored!

'Your brother, it seems, cares not for such entertainment, Sir Roger,' she said with an edge to her voice. 'Perhaps we should have consulted him first.'

Sir Gilbert's eyes rested on her thoughtfully. 'What you have provided will please the King. Isn't that all you need concern yourself with—my lady?'

The way he said 'my lady' implied that she hardly deserved the title. He might just as clearly have called her 'child'. Was that the reason for his inattention?

'Naturally. But from your wandering glance, I thought you might be expecting a troupe of dancing girls, hot-foot from Byzantium, to say the least.'

He smiled thinly, and Roger laughed. 'Ignore him, my lady, he cares only for the King's safety. Tell me instead of this bear. Have you seen it?'

'No, and I have no great desire to meet the creature. They

say it is of a great height and has already devoured two goats and four swine.'

'A worthy opponent,' Gilbert said thoughtfully. 'A beast of such size would provide rare sport for the King—and a warm bedcover after the kill besides.'

'The King has many such covers,' Roger said. 'Would he want another?'

'Maybe not, but as the bear is in the Beaumont demesne, perhaps the lady wishes to have first claim. Would it please you to have such a cover, my lady?' Did his tone hint at regret that the bear was on their land?

Alyce raised her chin and spoke firmly. 'Indeed it would. 'Twould make a most luxurious defence against the wind from the sea that cuts through my bedchamber. Should the King decline the skin, then I would be happy to accept it.'

Roger cast his brother a challenging look. 'Shall we contest for it, Gil? A wager with you. My new fur mantle against your jewelled dagger that my spear will put an end to this menace.'

'As to ends, we must allow that the bear may not be over-eager to lay down his life at the lady's behest.'

'Too cautious by half,' Roger said on a note of mockery. 'Where a lady's wish is concerned, one should dare all. You shall have your bearskin, lady, I promise, and I shall have Gilbert's dagger.'

'Or perhaps a corpse-cart in place of both.' Gilbert's voice held sardonic amusement and he glanced at Alyce. 'Brave words you are hearing, my lady, but rest easy. He has the skill—along with the desire to appear heroic.'

Roger grinned, his eyes dancing, and Alyce was enraptured by his bold spirit, one she felt sure would hurl itself joyously into the fray, never counting the cost. Privately she considered a daring knight the more romantic. To dare all was to win all. Everyone knew that!

LADY OF STARLIGHT 11

As they took their places at the long table with the King in the central place of honour, Alyce reflected that it was easy to tell the de Boveney brothers apart, as King William had said. They both had the darkly handsome Norman features and were of the same athletic build, but there the resemblance ended. While Gilbert was hard-eyed and looked on the world, it seemed, with cool cynicism, there was something in Roger she had never encountered before. A promise of adventure perhaps? A briefly-glimpsed view of an exciting new world? Whatever it was, her heart answered to him eagerly.

The silver water-basins were being brought round by liveried pages, and each guest's hands were washed and dried on scented napkins. At a nod from her father, Alyce filled the King's goblet with wine.

Her hands trembled a little, knowing those all-seeing eyes were on her. She looked up from her task. King William inclined his head and offered her the goblet in the Norman tradition of courtesy. She sipped from it and held it out to him, and he took it from her.

'Be well, mistress,' he said and drank deeply.

Alyce ate little, intent on seeing that all went well with their noble guest. A clumsy page who slopped a dish in his hurry was rebuked by a frown, and a lift of her finger to the ever-watchful steward-in-chief kept the King surrounded by the choicest dishes.

Course followed course while tumblers and jugglers skipped and cavorted before them: a ballad-singer mouthed extravagant verse to the warrior King under his sardonic gaze. As the meal progressed, the noise grew louder. Wine flowed and guests grew boisterous and bright-eyed. When an argument threatened to take a turn for the worse, the King's stare, cutting as a whiplash, rested harshly for a moment on the participants and they grew quiet. A dread King, thought Alyce, and yet his very starkness held men in his service for a lifetime. Not for love of him but out of respect, and the conviction that as a general he was without peer.

She knew his history from her father. Accepted by the nobles as legitimate heir of Normandy on the death of his father, Robert the third Duke, William's whole youth from that day, when he was only eight years old, had been woven through with danger and treachery. Invasion by France, greedy for conquest, rebellion from within the duchy itself, had forged in him a mind as sharp as a sword blade and a body that moved like whipcord. Not an inch of Normandy did he yield, and men grew to call him the Fighting Duke and Wolf of Normandy. But ambition beckoned, and he looked across from Normandy to Saxon England. That had been the heritage he intended for his sons.

Long before Alyce's time he had achieved his goal, which was why her home was here and not in Normandy. For men like her father who had followed the Duke, home was henceforth a castle to hold in his name. Earl Robert had sent for his French wife to join him. A few years later she had died, still hating this barbarian land that tore her away from the delights and cultures of Normandy.

But to Alyce who had known no other life, the hills and rivers, the marshes and harsh climate were home. The gulls wheeling out to sea, the north wind that raged through the castle, were as natural to her as the scented bowers and tapestried walls had been to her mother.

And so Edith, a Saxon widow, had arrived to care for her. Unlettered but wise in her way, she had taught Alyce the secrets of the herb-garden and how to spin and weave a fine length of cloth. For more intellectual lessons Alyce was tutored at the nearby convent, escorted there and back by her father's men-at-arms.

She jumped as the King spoke to her. 'Accept my compliments on your management, my lady. Earl Robert tells me you excel in all manner of arts. For one so young, that is high praise indeed.' He noted the slight rise of Alyce's chin and the darkening of her amber-coloured eyes, and a glint of amusement brightened his gaze. So—she resents my choice of word, he thought.

'I am not so young, Sire, for I am full sixteen.' She glanced at him as she spoke and recollected herself, blushing fiercely. 'But I thank you, Sire.'

'Tell me, my lady,' he said, giving her his full attention. 'You are of an age and beauty to be sought after by many men. Are you yet betrothed?'

'No, Sire,' she smiled ruefully into his face. 'My father has not yet spoken of this. He considers me, I believe, a child still.'

William laughed. 'I think he mistakes the matter too. We must look around for a fine husband for so excellent a maiden. I have many young men of good birth in my court. What think you of those here tonight?'

Alyce could not resist a fleeting glance towards the place where the de Boveney brothers sat. William's keen grey eyes noted the direction.

'Why, Sire,' she faltered, 'you have brought the—the chivalry of your court, I am sure. They—they are the noblest knights I have ever seen. But second only to yourself, of course, my liege.'

'Well said, mistress, but I promise you one of my finest young men for groom. A de Boveney, perhaps?' He smiled as she blushed. 'Let me think on it awhile.'

He turned to Earl Robert, and Alyce was free to converse with the gentleman on her left and to observe, as obliquely as she could, the side trestle of knights and their partners. She almost missed giving a polite reply to her neighbour as she watched Roger accept a sugared fruit from the long white fingers of a striking looking girl. He seemed perfectly happy in his flirtation and yet—her heart lifted suddenly—he glanced up, straight into her eyes and gave her a quick smile. She smiled back, and her bemused gaze passed on to Gilbert.

How grave he was, listening with every appearance of interest on his lean dark face to some story being recounted by an elderly Countess, a distant relative of her own. She could not fault his courtesy there but sensed it masked the boredom he felt on such occasions. There had been nothing specific in his conversation to which she could take exception, but there was about him an air of coolness, a hint of cruelty that was lacking in Roger. He was more like the King, she determined. Perhaps the same qualities of strength and ruthlessness had brought them together. As with the King she could imagine him to be a pitiless enemy. She withdrew her gaze with an inward shudder and turned back to her guest.

In an idle moment she glanced down the line of visitors at the top table. Beyond the King and her father were placed the nobles whose lands surrounded their own. It had only been courteous to invite them, and she had no complaint of their company but for one exception. Count Hubert de Louches was that exception.

He held a castle some two miles distant, his lands commencing beyond the river that divided their estates, and because of this proximity he visited them frequently. On the face of it there was no objection she could make, and as a child she had looked upon him merely as a guest and companion of her father. But of late she had found his eyes resting on her with more attention than a child merited. His jovial compliments and hearty kisses had seemed a trifle too extravagant for a man who was neither brother nor uncle. King William, reflected Alyce, was more astute than her father. She was no longer a child and did not wish to be petted like a child by male guests. Earl Robert saw no evil in such behaviour, but Alyce, in her burgeoning womanhood, disliked the way Count Hubert's damp lips lingered on her mouth or cheek and positively shuddered when he hugged her to his chest, his little eyes glistening as his strong fingers lingered on breast and hip. God help the girl, she thought suddenly, who found the Count a suitor for her hand. The vision of being locked in wifely passion with that one was too much to envisage.

Even his table manners roused her to disgust. As she watched him wipe the grease from his chin with the back of his hand, his glance swivelled and met her own. Colour swept her face as he licked his lips and grinned familiarly, then pursed his mouth in the semblance of a kiss.

A curt nod and she withdrew her gaze. Pray Heaven her father had not considered the possibility of a union between them! Or had he?

From that moment her neighbours found her a little preoccupied, her conversation a trifle disjointed. The King had shown an interest in her. Could she but foster that interest, then all might be safely resolved before, and if, Count Hubert approached her father. The decision of her betrothal must not be left to chance, for her father might consider a rich estate and high position of more importance than her own happiness.

The banquet, it seemed, went on for hours, but at last the ladies moved up the stairs to the solar, a room rich with tapestries, floor-rushes scented with rosemary and a great log fire. Here the female gossip took place, but Alyce, half-drugged by the heat and the excitement, asked leave to retire.

She left the solar and moved slowly down the stone steps of the spiral staircase, stifling a yawn. Her veil and headband she removed, and like a cloud of black silk, her hair fell free about her shoulders. What an exciting day it had been! First a meeting with King William of England, the man feared and dreaded by half of Europe. But to her he had been kind and courteous, acknowledging her as of marriageable age, not just as the child of his old friend.

Immune to flattery as he was, she must contrive to be sweetly submissive to his every whim in her efforts to retain his good opinion and be deemed worthy of marriage to one of his finest young men. Her lips curved in a reminiscent smile. One of his finest young men! Without doubt there was one who filled that bill admirably, one who had shown his interest by a challenge in her honour.

She swung round a corner of the stairway, her tasseled girdle flying as she jumped the last step. The flambeau set high in the wall threw shadows across the corridor leading to her room. She had taken but two steps in that direction when a bulky figure drew itself off the wall.

'My Lady Alyce is happy, it seems. She smiles and dances as if she guessed I should be waiting to kiss her goodnight.'

Alyce jumped and stopped dead, her smile fading. The man stepped out of the shadows and into the circle of light thrown by the wall torch. Count Hubert de Louches stood before her, his arms outstretched, barring her way.

'Come, little dove, and kiss me goodnight, then go to your virtuous couch and dream of me.'

'Please stand aside, sir, and allow me to pass.'

'What! Without a goodnight kiss? I knew you would not remain long with the ladies, so I determined to meet my little Alyce on her way to bed. Ah, would that I could accompany you—but be patient, my little one, for the time will come. Your father thinks you overly young as yet, but is not unaware of my interest. Me? I know when a maiden is ripe for bedding, my sweetness.'

Alyce strove to restrain the panic that rose in her. Sounds of laughter still drifted up from the banqueting hall, but the corridor and stairs were deserted.

'You are here as a guest, my lord, and I beg that you will allow me to retire to my room without hindrance.'

'Certainly, my dear, on payment of the toll. Is it too much

to ask? Just a little kiss from one whom I hold dear and hope to hold even dearer.'

'That day will never come, my lord. I am not your little Alyce and have never been so.'

Count Hubert's teeth glinted in the flame of the torch and he moved nearer.

'I admire your spirit, little lady. A show of reluctance is most seemly and delights a man.' His eyes travelled down her body, lingering on her neckline and the young unrestrained breasts rising and falling with her quick breathing. 'A fighting spirit is much to my taste, and I shall enjoy the mastering of you when we are wed.'

CHAPTER TWO

ALYCE threw caution to the winds. 'Wed!' she spat at him. 'To you? You revolt me with your pawings and wet kisses. Only out of deference to my father's guest did I ever let you come within ten miles of me. Your table manners would shame the untidiest pig in our sty. Marry you? I would rather take the tinker who lives in squalor beneath the castle wall.'

Count Hubert's face darkened. His hand shot out and gripped her wrist, dragging her close. 'Spine of God,' he growled, 'you will repent those words!'

She smelt the aroma of wine on his breath and saw the dark face, now blotched with anger, lean towards her.

'By my oath, I've a mind to take you this night and teach you the meaning of passion. You'll be glad then for the Earl to take me for son-in-law.'

Alyce strained away from him. 'Why would you bother with ceremony afterwards,' she flung at him, 'if 'tis only satisfaction you desire?'

'Should I take you penniless, little fool? Your father has no heir. What he possesses would come to me through you if 'twere legally done. And I doubt me not that shame would make you acquiescent, for who would want a maid who is no longer a maid?'

'You are mad. I have only to scream and my women will come running.'

'Women? Unarmed old women? Are they like to come at me with sword or dagger to preserve your virtue?'

Fool! Alyce told herself in rising horror. You have much to learn of men.

Far from convincing the Count that his suit was unwelcome and he should withdraw with honour, her scathing words had served only to incense him. Should he be mad enough to commit this deed, the damage would be done, her innocence defiled. What knight would accept a maid so despoiled?

Her mouth opened on a scream as Count Hubert's free hand swept aside an arras concealing a small alcove. Neither of them had heard a sound but suddenly a voice spoke, low and slightly drawling, but soft with menace.

'Unfortunately I left my sword below, but dagger I have and that will lose itself in your flesh if you do not release the girl at once.'

Count Hubert's fingers slackened on her wrist and Alyce dragged herself free and flung away from him, spinning round. For a moment she thought it was Roger and her heart leaped, but the hard eyes and menacing stare, together with the jewelled dagger, showed him for Sir Gilbert.

Count Hubert stared sideways in stunned disbelief at the man who had come upon them so silently. The long, glittering blade of the dagger rose and moved almost caressingly across the Count's thick neck. Sweat stood out on his forehead and a sickly pallor suffused his face.

For a very long moment, no one moved. Alyce held her breath, watching the slight scoring of Hubert's skin from which a few drops of blood trickled on to his tunic. Her gaze moved to the face of Sir Gilbert.

'What do you intend, Sir Gilbert?' she breathed.

Without looking at her, he said, 'The choice is yours, my lady. If you would like him tossed from the battlements, you have but to say the word.'

Alyce gasped, her eyes widening. She bit her finger, glancing swiftly at the Count. His bulging eyes showed that the threat was no idle one. Her hatred of him was such that she was tempted to say the word.

But Sir Gilbert—would he—dare he? She could well believe him capable of doing just that if the impulse took him.

With a sigh, she said, 'It would be less than he deserves, but not here, I think. Not in our bailey, I mean,' she explained as Gilbert flashed her a look. 'We must consider the King. It would not be in our best interests.'

'Very true—and at the same time—monstrous messy,' Gilbert said gravely, and Alyce had a strange feeling that he was enjoying himself. 'And if,' he added, 'I made of him a contender for your title of untidiest pig in the sty, this passageway would suffer a similar fate.' He raised an eyebrow. 'I feel his lordship to be overfull of blood to risk it.'

Count Hubert flinched away from the insistent blade. 'For the love of God, take that cursed dagger off my neck——!'

'Be quiet!' snapped Sir Gilbert. 'Give the lady time to decide what is to become of you. Only then may you show interest. Well, my lady? What choice do we have left?'

'I suppose,' said Alyce, genuine regret in her tone, 'that we must release him. After all, the King is here. His visit must remain pleasant.'

'There is that, of course. I commend your sound reasoning. But I'll have my men see him on his way home. You are free to go, Sir Pig, by the lady's benevolence.' He sheathed his dagger and stepped back. Count Hubert drew in a deep shaking breath. The look he bestowed on Gilbert was heavy with venom. 'I will remember this, de Boveney. Take care. As for you—you jade——' He glared at Alyce from bloodshot eyes.

There was a hiss as Gilbert's dagger slid from its sheath again. 'Go quickly, Count, before I revoke the lady's wish. It would be most unwise to bandy words at this point.'

Although Gilbert spoke quietly and without emphasis,

there was a hint of menace in his voice, far more terrifying than if the words had been flung out in anger. Count Hubert paled and his eyes moved uneasily to the jewelled dagger.

There was a clatter from the steps below and round the corner swung two knights of the King, laughing and talking. They fell silent as they came across the group. Gilbert's dagger was already sheathed, but his face still held a dangerous look.

'Your pardon, my lady, my lords,' said one, bowing. 'We go to clear our heads on the battlements. 'Tis a strong ale you brew here, my lady.' He smiled at Alyce.

'Oh, Gaston—a favour before you proceed,' interposed Sir Gilbert. 'Count de Louches has been called home quite suddenly. I would deem it a service if you and young Roland would escort him to the castle gate and see him on his way. May I entrust that task—safely—to you?'

Gaston regarded Sir Gilbert keenly, then nodded. 'It shall be as you wish, my friend.'

'But surely,' protested Roland, 'the Count knows in which direction——'

'Hold your tongue, halfling,' interrupted Gaston on a jocular note. 'And attend the wishes of your betters. Sir Gilbert stands high with the King. Do you seek to question his orders?'

'N-no, of course not.'

''Tis well an you wish to retain your newly-won spurs. Come, my lord Count, accept our escort to the gates.'

Without a word Count Hubert fell into step between the two knights and they clattered down the stairs and out of sight, Gaston still indulging in a flow of humorous admonitions on knightly conduct to the young Roland.

As the sounds died away, Alyce bent to retrieve her veil and headband, dropped in the struggle. She raised her eyes to Sir Gilbert, suddenly aware of the unbound hair spilling about her shoulders.

'Forgive my disarray, sir,' she murmured, her cheeks pink with embarrassment. 'I was on the point of retiring when I was waylaid by that—that——'

'Pig?' he offered.

'Exactly! But perhaps that is not a fair description.' She frowned.

'Of the Count?' he asked, amazed.

'Of our pigs, sir, for they are really very clean beasts and quite lovable.' She gave an expressive shudder. 'How dare he suppose I would welcome his advances? Oh, but I forget my manners, Sir Gilbert. I thank you most heartily for your welcome intervention, but I feel you have made an enemy on my account.'

'Count Hubert and I have crossed paths before, my lady, and no doubt will do so again, so there is no need to hold yourself to blame, for we are already enemies. I am glad you suffered no hurt at his hands, for his reputation is not of the highest in his dealings with your sex.' He paused and added, musingly, 'But I had not imagined him to have sunk so low as to molest children.'

Alyce stared at him, her eyes widening, and in their depths he read a spark of rising indignation. Her slight figure stiffened, her lips parted as her colour deepened. She gazed at him with an icy hauteur.

He was quite unused to such looks, and his temper rose in consequence. His glance raked her from top to toe, from the fall of hair to the hem of her gown. God's teeth, he swore savagely, the pride of the child! Did she think he had rushed to the rescue for the sake of her maidenly virtue? This crossing of swords with de Louches was the only diversion in an evening of boredom. She had been merely the spark that lit the fuse.

'I cannot commend your handling of the Count,' he countered harshly through clenched teeth. 'You should know better than to inflame one of his stamp with insults. Have you learned nothing of men? He asked only a kiss. Are they so precious that a man must kneel and beg with flowery compliments for such an honour to be bestowed upon him? You rate your youthful charms higher than they merit, let me tell you.'

'How dare you speak in that way to me!'

'How dare you look upon me with such disdain! As if I were an insolent page.'

'Had you been a page, I should have boxed your ears,' she flung at him.

'Am I to thank my station in life for such forbearance, then?' he mocked. 'God's teeth, child, you have much to learn before you can call yourself lady.'

Alyce's fury boiled over. Her hand flew out and the slap that landed on his cheek was like a crack of thunder in the silent corridor.

Sir Gilbert stood very still. His fingers, clenched into fists, held tightly to his sides. The mark of her hand showed starkly against his suddenly pale skin.

Alyce stared into his face, appalled by her action. Something glowed in the depths of his eyes, something cold and deadly. She was unable to break away from his look. Her bones were like ice. It was a long time before he spoke.

'Any but the child of my host would have paid with his life for that,' he said, and the words seemed to fall with a blood-chilling clarity from the mask of his face. 'But I will teach you a lesson you will not forget in a hurry. You may even be improved by it.' His arms reached for her. 'I would prefer to whip you until you begged for mercy, but instead I will take that which you hold to be so precious.'

She felt herself pulled roughly into his arms. His grip was so tight she cried out, but the cry was cut short as his mouth fastened on hers. He kissed her fiercely, expertly, and with a violence that roused terror in her. His lips moved over her face, her neck and the skin above her neckline. Her struggles were useless, she was pinned against his breast as if in a vice. Count Hubert's kisses had revolted her but Sir Gilbert's were different, hot and dry, but terrifying because of their ferocity and strength.

He lifted his head once to stare into her eyes as she gasped for breath.

'For pity's sake, sir, release me,' she begged. 'I am sorry for striking you and ask your forgiveness.'

'Release you?' he asked mockingly. 'I think you have not yet paid enough for that folly. Perhaps I will continue where Count Hubert left off.' He saw the blood leave her face and felt her body go limp in his arms.

Her voice came in a whisper. 'You would not! You could not be so base as to——to rape me in my own home.'

His arms fell away so suddenly that she staggered. He stared into the face grown ashen beneath the cloud of dark hair. 'I don't rape children,' he answered coldly, 'your virtue is safe with me. But when next you meet de Louches, spare a thought for the virtue of those on his estate who have no protection. Guard that viper's tongue of yours, or you may not be so lucky next time.'

Alyce fled down the corridor, relief and humiliation vying with hatred.

His gaze followed her, his hard eyes contemplative, until she turned into a room, then he gave a wry smile and shook his head. Perhaps he had gone too far, but she deserved the fright he had given her. That haughty look of hers had stung him into retaliation.

He surprised himself by grinning suddenly. By Our Lady, she was a proud one! As proud, he admitted ruefully, as himself. But she had spirit and breeding, a good combination. Had she been a grown woman, unrelated to the household, wise in dalliance, who knew but what he might have enjoyed a more fitting reward for his rescue from the Count?

But a virgin child? Ah, no, that was not to his taste. He was no Count Hubert to take by force. It had never been necessary.

He continued on his way up to the battlements. As Gaston had remarked, the Beaumont ale was strong and, although he was not a great drinker, Gilbert had felt the need for fresh air himself on leaving the great hall. Like the King he was a temperate man, his pleasures to be found more in the field than in the banqueting halls of the nobility. There had been women, naturally, for no man is a saint, but those with whom he had sported had all been experienced in the art, meeting passion with passion, acknowledging no permanence. His heart had never been touched. He doubted it ever would be.

Alyce, meanwhile, lay in bed, anger raging through her. She would never forgive Gilbert de Boveney for the shameful way he had treated her. Her lips felt burned and bruised by his kisses. She had almost believed—but no, he had meant only to teach her a lesson, nothing more; but her fear had been real.

She shivered, remembering his ferocity. As the heat cooled in her, she realised that in part, she had brought it upon herself. But that was no excuse for handling her so brutally. She hated him wholeheartedly. Was it in him to be gentle—even to one he loved? And should that one reject him—what then? A conquest by force? A dire prospect indeed for any woman!

She drowsed deep in her bed of fine linen, flung over with the soft stitched pelts of animals, and wished it had been Roger who had routed Count Hubert. Even as she thought of him she realised that the choice of husband lay in the hands of Earl Robert. One did not defy one's own father, but she felt he might be guided by the King who had followed his own heart, after all. And if she were clever enough to intimate her choice to His Majesty, then all might be arranged satisfactorily.

It was well known that King William, while still Duke of Normandy, had said on first laying eyes on the Lady Matilda, daughter of Earl Baldwin of Flanders, that he must have her for wife. And what a stormy courtship that had been! A strange relationship of two strong-willed people fighting for mastery, and no one quite knowing whether it was love or hate that bound them.

But proud Matilda, conscious of her superior birth, had finally been mastered by the Duke. And yet in her own time and in her own way she had surrendered, binding him to her even closer. He called her witch, for the spell she had cast never weakened, even to her death. Alyce sighed deeply, and her cheek sank on to the soft skins.

From the parapet of the keep the next morning, she watched the royal party assemble for the hawking. Squires scurried across the bailey, their lord's colours singing clear in the sunlight and tiny pages, tabards flying ran in and out of the throng bringing forgotten mantle brooches and the occasional cap for the older man. Most went bare-headed and were clean-shaven in the Norman manner but a number were now adopting the English style of flowing hair and beards. The falconers were crossing the bailey from the mews, a hooded bird jessed to each wrist.

Alyce watched the unhurried transfer of the short strap of her father's favourite bird from the falconer to the King. The curving talons gripped and settled on the scarred leather of his heavy gauntlet glove, and the King raised his wrist. The breeze ruffled the slate-grey feathers and the falcon's head went up as if scenting the coming chase.

Her gaze passed over the dozen or so mounted men and came to rest on a small group of knights behind the King. She saw the glint of chainmail beneath their cloaks and noted the conical helmets resting on the saddle pommels. Although the King was out for pleasure, the men of his bodyguard went armed and ready, for the kingdom still simmered with sporadic unrest.

King William threw a remark over his shoulder and the riders formed up behind him, helmets in place, the straight nasal guards almost disguising their features. But she could recognise the de Boveney brothers, although not able to distinguish one from the other except perhaps by the flash of a grin which was more likely to be Roger. Gilbert's smile did not hold the same frankness, his was half-mocking, making one feel young and selfconscious, but Roger's smile was open, his eyes clear and revealing as the windows of the chapel through which the sun streamed, bright and pure.

The King's stallion leapt forward and the straining horses swept after it, galloping across the beaten earth and thundering over the wooden drawbridge with a sound that set the hens squawking in the barn and the stabled destriers pounding in their stalls. Alyce watched as they crested the hill, mantles and standards streaming in the breeze of their passing until all had merged into the faint haze.

Even after their departure, the castle grounds resounded with noise. The stands for seating guests at the tournament tomorrow were not yet finished, and the great striped marquees for housing competitors with their squires and armourers were still being hauled into place. But she had no time to watch the activity. Her father would expect a mountain of roast meats to be ready on the return of the hunting party. The temper of a hungry man was apt to be alarming, and she dare not risk his displeasure when she must needs keep him sweet to further the scheme she had in mind. Just how she was to achieve it was still a little vague, but the most important part was to win the King to her cause.

She heard the huntsmen return amidst a great noise and flew down the steps to meet them. The servants, she noted briefly and with satisfaction, were staggering into the hall with great trenchers of steaming meats and jugs of ale. Before she could reach the outer doors she was met by her own page, Ranulf, white of face and wide-eyed with fear.

'My lady,' he gasped. 'The King——'

'The King?' she asked sharply. 'What has happened?'

'He—he—sends for you, my lady.'

'He is hurt, Ranulf? Tell me quickly.'

'No, lady, not that.' He gulped, casting a scared look over his shoulder. 'He requests that you go quickly, for he has something of import to say to you in the bailey. My lady——' He hesitated. 'He is looking most fearsome. Take care, for the love of God.'

Alarmed by his words, Alyce ran swiftly down the outer steps into the courtyard and stared about her, her eyes wide with apprehension. How had she offended? The men were gathered in a circle which opened as she moved towards it. King William stood in the centre with his arms folded, and spread before him on the ground was an animal skin.

The reddish brown fur, already stripped from the beast, was stained dark red in places. She regarded it doubtfully. It could be a deer.

Her heart grew suddenly cold. A red deer or hind from the King's preserve, belonging only to the Crown and forbidden to the common people? She had heard how the King loved his deer; almost, some said, as though he were their father. She had heard too of the law relating to their slaying by the peasants. The penalty was to be blinded!

But what, her mind asked in stricken panic, had it to do with her? How was she to be blamed? Had it been a servant, caught in the act? Was that it? One of her own servants?

She raised her eyes fearfully. 'Sire, you sent for me?' She looked into William's face. His eyes were fixed on her in a stare that froze her bones. Was this the face his enemies saw, this stark, merciless mask? She was suddenly afraid.

CHAPTER THREE

ALYCE faced the King. 'Sire,' she said faintly, 'I am here as you commanded.'

Her eyes were drawn to the skin again. If it was indeed a red deer, then her dream of the King's continuing interest was lost. Her gaze sharpened. The fur was coarse, too coarse, surely, for a deer? Hope stirred as a glimmer of understanding rose, slackening her fear. Her gaze came up in relief.

'You killed the bear, Sire?'

'Not I,' he said, frowning in displeasure. 'This is de Boveney's work. I had promised myself a fine quarry, but it seems my will was flouted by the Lady Alyce's need of a bedcovering, I am told. What have you to say to that?'

She gave a gasp, her eyes flinching away from the stern face for a moment, then her head came up and she met the hard stare with a steady look. She thought of Roger's determination to win the wager and was afraid for him. He had acted rashly and without thought just to please her, she was convinced. To keep his promise he had unwittingly roused the King to anger. He must not suffer for her sake.

'I crave pardon, Sire, for the knight and myself. It was but a politeness to me, for Sir Gilbert deemed the bear in our demesne. Their talk of contest arose from high spirits only, for who would knowingly incur Your Majesty's displeasure on my account? The skin is yours, my liege, with my deepest respect and sorrow for your loss.'

'How then shall I punish the one who robbed me of this kill?'

'Beau Sire, forgive him,' she beseeched. 'I swear he knew not your own wish, or he would have stayed his hand. In the heat of the chase emotions run high, as I am sure Your Majesty will know. He would not defy Your Grace for my sake.'

The grey eyes looked keenly into hers, then the King's face softened. 'A lucky knight it is to have a lady plead his cause with such fervour. Fear not, mistress, I was but jesting. I never saw a better placed spear, for the beast turned and attacked in desperation. I cannot rebuke a knight for such skill for I was in its path myself. The prize is yours, and may you have pleasant dreams beneath your new bedcover.'

He laughed, the nobles around him joining in, and Alyce realised that his anger had been assumed for her benefit. To see if she was worthy of betrothal to a knight of his court? she wondered.

Under cover of the noise, the King moved close and murmured, 'Your championship does you credit, lady. If you can stand against me for the sake of the knight yonder,' he jerked his head in the direction of the stables, 'then my promise holds, and I will not delay in speaking to your father. You have my royal word on it.'

He signed to the servants and they dragged away the skin.

Alyce curtsied deeply and withdrew from his presence as her father led the King into the great hall. She glanced across at the stables. A tall figure was moving towards them and she started forward eagerly, reaching him before realising it was Gilbert. It was too late to retreat.

'Sir, where is your brother?' she asked with determined unconcern.

He gazed at her lazily and indicated the interior of the stable. 'His squire is attending an injury he sustained.' His glance was completely impersonal.

Alyce clasped her hands tightly. 'He was wounded in the chase?'

'A slight scratch only. A shade too near a claw, but that is ever Roger's way. Rash in all things.' He spoke mockingly and she bit back a sharp retort, forcing herself to play the role without emotion.

'His Majesty is rather terrifying, isn't he? I feared for the life of your brother.'

A slight frown appeared on Gilbert's brow. 'How so, my lady?'

'The King spoke harshly of being robbed of the bear kill. I was afraid he intended to punish Sir Roger severely, but I should have known he was jesting for who would punish a knight for saving the King from injury? I pleaded with him to withhold, for I did not realise the King himself was hoping to kill the bear.' She looked at him with sudden suspicion. 'Did you, sir?'

'Acquit me, lady, of knowing the King's mind. But he spoke of it, yes.'

'And you held to the wager, knowing that Roger was determined to win?'

The hard eyes held a suddenly inscrutable look. 'As I said before, Roger is rash. Does that not please you when it is for your sake?'

'Not if it brings him into conflict with the King. Although he promised—it would not have signified—I would not have cared——' She stopped abruptly, reddening under his quizzical gaze.

'I was not with the King just now,' he said, 'but your remarks are beginning to make sense. I surmise you are come to congratulate the victor?'

'Yes, of course. Will you take me to your brother, sir? I have some skill with wounds and must attend him immediately.'

He led her into a stable recess where Roger was sitting on a stool, his squire beside him tearing up strips of linen. The sleeve of Roger's tunic had been slit to the elbow and Gilbert's jewelled dagger lay at his feet.

The wound was not deep but Alyce had just the cure. She sent the squire running to her small herb-cupboard for mortar and pestle and a certain jar of herbs newly gathered. As she pulped the leaves, stalk and flowers of Golden Rod, she explained to a doubting Roger that most assuredly this mixture would cleanse any wound and prevent infection. She had never known it to fail, in fact it had arrested bleeding in far more serious cases than his.

' 'Tis more powerful than comfrey or St John's wort, though if you wish to repel demons at the same time, I would advise St John's wort.'

She looked up into Roger's dancing eyes. 'No demons, lady, save the one behind you. Go away, Gil, and feed your horse or something. We shall manage better without you. I am in good hands and not likely to die under such delicate ministering.'

Alyce glanced over her shoulder at Gilbert. 'Have no fear, sir, I have healed many wounds. As for this unfeeling brother of yours, I advise you to punish him yourself and add to his hurts by taking back your jewelled dagger.' She bent to fix the poultice in place before winding the linen strips round Roger's arm.

'Jewelled dagger?' asked Roger. 'Ah, yes, the one you used to ruin my tunic with, Gil.' He looked ruefully at the tattered sleeve. 'What of it?'

'It seems the King complained to my lady of being robbed of the bear kill and threatened to punish the one responsible,' Gilbert told him, leaning his back on the stable door and folding his arms.

Roger's brows shot up. 'He was angered?'

'Not too seriously, I gather, but the lady was not to know

that.' He regarded his brother with a smile glinting in his eyes. 'The Lady Alyce spoke in your defence right prettily. You should be flattered that she feared for you because of your victory in the contest.'

'Ah, yes, that wager we made,' Roger murmured. 'I had forgotten in the excitement of the kill.'

'Not so, my Lady Alyce. What do you say to that?'

Roger picked up the dagger. He balanced it on the palm of his hand, moving it to catch the sun's rays, then with a quick movement tossed it to Gilbert. His brother caught it deftly. Roger's eyes rested caressingly on Alyce's downbent head, then rose to meet the quizzing look from the dark-eyed man at the door.

Gilbert laughed. 'Are you refusing the spoils of victory?'

Roger glanced down at Alyce, his expression tender. 'Let us not hold to the terms. I need only the lady's esteem. Will you accept it?'

'For your sake?'

'And the lady's.'

Gilbert nodded and thrust the dagger into its sheath. 'Perhaps it will serve,' he murmured, and turned on his heel.

Alyce watched him walk away and then turned shining eyes on Roger. 'That was generous of you to return his dagger. I am sure he would not have shown such generosity to you.'

Roger rose, drawing her to her feet. 'It seems your opinion of Gil is not high, my lady.'

'I am sorry, I should not criticise your brother. It is just that he has a manner so hard and distant that he frightens me a little. He also,' she added, frowning in displeasure, 'treats me as if I were a child, which I am not.'

'That fact, my lady, has not gone unnoticed by me. Take no heed of Gil, his tastes are not mine.'

He smiled, lifting her chin with one long finger. 'He has no appreciation for beautiful maidens with amber eyes that are brighter than the jewels in his dagger. Or are they more like stars that glow in the midnight of your hair? How I should love to see your tresses unbound.'

Alyce's gaze fell under the ardent look. 'Perhaps you will one day, Sir Roger.'

'I wish I could look forward to that day, but after this visit of the King, your castle will be swarming with suitors for your hand when news of your beauty spreads abroad—you will overlook my devotion in the rush of noble claimants. Or can you, perhaps, keep in a little corner of your heart my own, which was lost on our meeting?'

'Not just a little corner, Sir Roger, for I shall remember you most tenderly.'

Roger took her gently by the shoulders. 'Alyce, my lady, I thank you for those words, and for the kind deed you have just performed.'

'I trust your arm will feel easier presently, sir.'

'My arm will heal, but never my heart.'

Alyce had never heard such words before. Her heart melted before their beauty, and her gaze on the knight was radiant. 'Oh, Roger,' she said with feeling. 'How I wish it had been you last night.'

'Last night?' His voice sharpened. 'What of last night?'

'Sir Gilbert did not mention it, then? I am glad, for I would not have it public knowledge.'

'Alyce! What happened? Did Gil——?' His expression was so hard that she pressed her hands against his chest, delighting in the feel of the beating heart, so like her own.

'Sir Gilbert rescued me from Count de Louches, who was angry when I refused his advances. Your brother chanced along the corridor at the most opportune moment. I am grateful to him for that, for the Count was bent on evil.'

'I see,' he said slowly. 'I know of de Louches and his habits. I wish I had been there.'

'You were still in the banqueting hall, I expect.'

LADY OF STARLIGHT 35

'No, I had ridden out to take a look at your village.'

'At night?'

He smiled. 'Haven't you noticed that things are more beautiful at night? A mysterious world under a cloak of starlight and shadows. The banquet became fatiguing, so I went out to seek the air. Do you always retire so early?'

'No, but I was tired after so much preparation for the visit.'

'Then I must take the air in another direction tonight.'

Alyce felt a rising excitement but controlled it, saying demurely, 'You did not appear fatigued while your partner was feeding you sugared fruits.'

Roger laughed. 'The lady was too obvious and patently bored with her own spouse. I play the game but only so far. With you so distant and the King beside you, I dared not stare at you all night as my heart wished.'

'You flatter me too much. Am I a part of your game, too?'

She waited for his reply, her heart beating agonisingly. Was such talk just idle diversion to this knight of the court, or could she believe he spoke in truth?

For reply he bent and kissed her swiftly on the lips, his arms holding her in a tight embrace.

'I play no game with you, my Alyce——' He broke off as the sound of heavy footsteps reached them. His arms dropped and he stepped back, bowing formally as a squire clattered into the stable. 'May I escort you into the hall, my lady?' His eyes were warm, his smile rueful.

Alyce shook her head. 'I must return these things to the herb store, sir. Please go on, or they will miss you.' She gathered up her pots and jars as swiftly as her trembling fingers allowed and left the stable.

It was cool in the stone-walled herb store. She needed time to regain her poise and still the excited fluttering of her heart. Could it be that love and duty lay in the same direction? The choice of husband was one decided by her father. No girl was ever asked her opinion. Rank and possession were the only considerations, and a girl must accept the man chosen. If one was ill-favoured and brought no dowry, thereby receiving no offers, only then was it permitted to remain single or take the veil. But the de Boveneys were a noble family and stood well with the King, and the King had looked kindly upon her. If he suggested the match, her father would not object.

Alyce laid her warm cheek against the stonework, her mind full of golden daydreams. Roger was so open in his admiration, his words as sincere as any could wish. It was a courtship after her own heart, and with the King's promise, there could be no possible reason for her father to find cause against it.

When she entered the hall for the midday meal, the King gave her a special smile, his grey eyes twinkling. She smiled in return. It was as if between them a secret bond was forged. They both knew what others didn't and Alyce was content, for her faith in the King was implicit. She never for a moment doubted that all would come to pass as he had promised. His royal word was enough.

The King and her father, together with others of his court, fell into a discussion on hawking and the merits of various lures used to induce the hawk to return to its handler. Alyce listened idly, immersed in her own thoughts. When the King declared his intention of hunting across the hills with only a chosen few, he turned to her and said with a command in his voice, 'And I look to you, my lady, to entertain our younger knights, for I refuse to have a crowd about me on this hunt. I will not again be thwarted and so I tell you. Take the de Boveneys off my hands and 'twill be to our mutual benefit, mistress. Ride where you will, but keep to the lowland, or I will not be so lenient next time.'

He frowned fiercely at her and she gave him a shining glance, her lips curving into a smile. He might ask the earth from her and she would obey most gladly. 'It shall be as you command, my lord King. None shall leave my side, for I shall so instruct my own escort of trusted men.'

A number of guests remained at the castle, venturing their skill at archery on the butts beyond the bailey. After watching the direction the King's party took as they left the castle, Alyce gathered the knights together. The de Boveneys, with Gaston and Roland beside them, together with a small company of Beaumont men-at-arms, prepared for a ride across country to the village. Far enough from the hills, Alyce decided, to avoid interference with the royal party, for it lay some miles south towards the sea but near enough to the castle for a leisurely ride. Edith had said it was a market day, so there would be some entertainment for her guests.

The sun beat down from a high clear sky, as blue as a Saxon's eyes. The breeze was slight, teasing the fringed trappings of her palfrey and the blue veil that shimmered and skirled behind her dark head. They cantered over the drawbridge, and once on the grass Roger drew abreast of her.

She knew without looking that it was he for she heard his soft laugh. In her own time she turned and glanced into the eyes regarding her. For some reason she thought of Queen Matilda, beloved of the King, and kept her gaze cool. He must not be too sure, she decided, for a man will reach farther for the less attainable. The Lady Matilda had already been widowed when she had met William, Duke of Normandy. Alyce had no such experience to assist in her knowledge of men, but even in her youth she was wise enough to remember Roger's remark about the girl by his side at the first banquet.

Too obvious, he had said. A man had no interest in the obvious, his instincts were those of the hunter. The quarry must present a challenge, not an easy target. That which was taken by conquest was of greater value. The King had known it in his pursuit of Matilda.

So be it. Roger must find her a little less eager for his

company. Like Matilda she must blow hot and cold to retain his regard until he had eyes and thoughts for no one else.

And so her smile was friendly and she drew both Gaston and the young Roland to her side, pointing out the old Saxon battlegrounds and the strange burial mounds they called barrows. Sir Gilbert rode behind, silent but watchful, while the Beaumont men-at-arms cantered in a wide circle about them, their eyes searching the countryside for hidden dangers. They were armed and armoured, for one never knew when a roving band of ruffians might appear to attack the travellers. Although the King had made great strides by his harsh treatment of robbers, there was still the occasional band of ex-soldiers or runaway serfs to menace travellers in the more inaccessible places.

Before they reached the village, Alyce had become on easy terms with Gaston, who kept her amused by his quips, and even young Roland, so newly knighted and still a little in awe of the older men, had overcome his shyness of her. He almost forgot, in the joy of conversing with one even younger than himself, that she was an Earl's daughter and the hostess of his King.

With these two and Roger all vying for her attention, the ride seemed short and Sir Gilbert completely forgotten. It was not until they had reached the one street, dusty and uneven, running between a collection of thatched cottages, that Sir Gilbert spoke. He moved ahead and motioned the men-at-arms to close in about their mistress.

'There is an air of something amiss here, my lady,' he said, meeting her eyes and understanding with a slight twist of his lips the indignation she felt at his ordering of her men.

'I see no reason for your fear, Sir Gilbert,' she retorted coldly, her chin rising. 'It is the market day and a time of excitement for the villagers. Why should that alarm you?'

'You have not been looking into their faces, my lady. There is more than excitement in them. There is fear too, and the hopeless anger that falls on those who cannot escape what is happening in their midst.'

He looked at Gaston and their eyes met in some kind of signal. Gaston drew ahead too, saying over his shoulder, 'Stay close to the lady, Roland, and loose your sword. I, also, feel something in the air that I mislike.'

'And will you too desert me, Roger?' Alyce asked sharply. 'For some imaginery danger?'

Roger had been frowning after Gaston and Gilbert, and the face he turned to her had lost its laughter. 'My eyes have not been on the peasants, but when Gil scents danger, I attend. Do not belittle the feeling, Alyce, for Gil has fought beside the King in the north and the far west more than any other knight. He seems to have the second sight where treason and ambush lurk.'

He too loosened his sword in its scabbard, glancing over at Roland. 'Let us hope this is not your baptism of fire, lad,' he said on a smile, but his expression was thoughtful and his gaze scanned the cottages keenly.

They had been following slowly the two mounted figures whose swords, now unsheathed, lay across their pommels. The track widened and opened to reveal the stalls of market produce set in a rough circle. Goats and cows stood tethered. There was a mendicant in friar's robes, his hands clasped tightly together below the rough frieze of his sleeves. Beside him stood the pedlar, his wares of ribbon and cloth, braid and girdles lying spread upon the ground about his pack.

Alyce was on the point of remarking in blighting accents that Sir Gilbert's second sight had deserted him on this occasion, when she became aware of the uncanny silence. No bartering or good-humoured haggling was taking place. The friar and pedlar were motionless. The merchants were missing from their stalls.

Gaston and Sir Gilbert had stopped. Their eyes, like everyone else's, were directed to the centre of the market square. People, both sellers and buyers, were all staring in one direction. Peasants passed Alyce's party, hurrying to the square. It was true; the faces held fear and barely concealed anger. They exchanged no words, and the air was heavy with resentment.

Alyce urged the palfrey forward. In God's name, she wondered, what was happening? Her escort closed up, forming a solid body around her. Drawing abreast of Sir Gilbert, she stared too, trying to discover the meaning of this unusual display. At first she could see nothing to explain the tightly-packed group between the stone church and the moot-hall; then, as two tall helmeted figures moved from one foot to another, she glimpsed between and understood.

The stocks and whipping-post, erected many years ago and scarred by use in the early days of William's harsh rule, stood before the manor court, or moot-hall, as the English called it. They were not much used these days, for the language problem was less. In the beginning the Normans had taken for disobedience the inability of the peasantry to understand their orders, and punishments had been freely given. The villagers had had little Latin apart from the odd word from their priest, and no French. Few Normans had spoken English, and their impatience and conviction that they dealt with a race of ignorant, obstinate people resulted in a rule of terror, completely without comprehension to the villagers. But in time the Normans had learned the tongue and the English and French languages became a mixture of both, understood on each side.

The whipping-post, some six feet high, was, on this sunny afternoon, the focus of all eyes. A pair of sunburned but slender wrists were being bound close to the highest point.

Alyce rose in her stirrups to obtain a better view, and her gaze moved down the arms. Some stable lad or young groom, she supposed, had inflicted harm on a knight's horse, those pampered beasts fed on the best corn and housed in more comfort than their human attendants.

Her gaze halted abruptly. The long flowing hair, the colour of early wheat, belonged to no stable lad. Her low exclamation of surprise and the sudden flash of her amber eyes brought a swift reaction from Gilbert.

He laid a hand on her bridle. 'Softly, lady.'

She stared at him. 'That is a girl tied there! What crime can a girl commit to be whipped in public?'

'Who knows? But is it our business? This land is not, I think, in your father's holding.'

'No. It is mostly free-held by farmers and tenant households.'

'To whom do the tenants pay their rents?'

'I believe,' Alyce said slowly and frowning in thought, 'that a few hides are glebe land and so those tenants will pay to the church, most likely in labour service. Yes—I am almost sure the Abbey owns this land on which the village is built.'

'Then we are not in some other lord's demesne?'

'I think not.' Her gaze had travelled half-unseeingly across the heads of the crowd. The two tall soldiers had turned, their pikes held horizontally, forcing back the villagers.

'Then,' said Gilbert, 'we are entitled to approach and see what it is that agitates the people so much that they must needs be held back. Some small crime like a cheating merchant would arouse derision and approval from them, but this is something they resent.' He removed his hand from her bridle and turned to Gaston, murmuring a few low-voiced words. Gaston nodded and jerked his head at Roland and the escort.

CHAPTER FOUR

WITH Gilbert and Roger on either side of her, Alyce moved her palfrey forward. The villagers parted willingly to allow them passage. Alyce was known to them, and Earl Robert had the reputation of being a good lord to his people. Her own servant, Edith, was of this village too, and none could say that Edith's devotion arose from fear. They welcomed Alyce with hope in their faces; they trusted her, for was she not a high-born lady who would understand and explain this thing to them?

Alyce read the hope and wondered what they expected of her.

'She is innocent, my lady,' they whispered. 'She is a good maid and the charge—whatever it is—is false.'

The three of them had reached the centre and were now able to see what was going forward. The pikemen looked up warily, but Alyce sensed a certain unease in their glances. Then she stared at the prisoner. The fair head was drooping, but through the curtain of her hair her eyes were fixed on a soldier facing towards her. The man was young and erect, but his face caught Alyce's attention.

Unlike the others, he was unarmed. He looked sick and white, his lips tightly compressed, but he was watching the girl with an agonised expression. Close behind him stood another soldier. Why so close? Alyce wondered. Then as the young man swayed momentarily, the one behind grasped his arm quickly and jerked him upright. But Alyce had seen. In that parting second the sun had glinted on steel, the spark swiftly obliterated by the close contact again. The young soldier was being forcibly restrained from any interference by the dagger at his back.

She looked at Roger. He was leaning forward on the pommel of his saddle, idly regarding the girl, then he glanced at Alyce. 'A pretty wench—a shame to see that white skin striped. What can her crime be, I wonder?'

The creak of a saddle made Alyce look towards Sir Gilbert. His hard eyes were scanning the area. He seemed satisfied by what he saw and turned again, meeting her glance.

'Did you see?' she asked softly, her eyes resting briefly on the young soldier. He might have noticed, being nearer than Roger.

He nodded. 'I caught the glint of it, but wait until we know the strength of them.' His look passed on to Roger. 'Not more than six, would you say?'

Roger agreed. 'By my count too, unless there are more inside.' He nodded towards the manor court building.

'We shall soon see,' replied Gilbert, 'for here comes the instigator of the whole affair, I would imagine. Keep your tongue between your teeth, my lady,' he warned, 'until we know more of this.'

Alyce followed the direction of his gaze and was so taken aback that she had no breath to rebuke him for his insolence. Count Hubert de Louches stepped out from the moot-hall, his small eyes glittering in anticipation. Only two men attired in his livery followed. The Count had cast aside his jerkin and rolled up the sleeves of his shirt; his thick hairy arms were bared to the sun and his muscles bulged as he swung a heavy thonged whip negligently.

Alyce gazed in horror as he flicked the whip back and forth, catching the end with a hand that was hard and calloused. His eyes were only for the girl, he ignored the villagers and the hiss of indrawn breath from a score of throats. His free hand reached out and ripped the cotton bodice from neck to waist, exposing the slender back and white skin. The girl gasped and her cheek pressed tightly to the post, her eyes closing.

The Count waited, dragging out the moment of suspense into an eternity.

'Are you ready, wench?' he finally asked. 'Or does the thought of what is to come persuade you to a wiser course? You have only to ask pardon and swear to serve me willingly, and freedom is yours.'

There was no answer from the girl and the Count cracked the whip idly. She flinched but made no sound. The thick arm rose. The crowd moved but the pikemen were ready, thrusting them back. A heavy silence descended.

Into that silence came a voice, lightly mocking, but rising in tone with bell-like clarity. 'My lord Count,' said Roger, one elbow resting lazily on his pommel, 'hold a moment. Before you proceed with this somewhat unusual entertainment, may we know—as late arrivals on the scene—the events leading up to this punishment?'

The words spun away into the silence like echoes of a chapel bell. The Count had started violently at the first note. He stared over at the speaker and his face darkened. ''Tis none of your business.'

Glancing at Roger, Alyce saw the light of joy in his eyes. It was his left arm she noted too, that leaned on the pommel. The right rested on his sword-hilt.

'Then make us privy to the secret, my lord,' Roger went on, 'for entertainment without comprehension is less amusing. If what you intend is enjoyable to you, then let us understand and share your joy.'

Count Hubert's glance took in Alyce and Sir Gilbert, and behind them the crowd. His eyes grew smaller with cunning and a smile hovered on his lips. They were alone, it seemed, and in no position to upset his plans.

'Your guests have no right of interference here, my lady. You are out of your demesne.'

'But so are you, my lord,' Gilbert said silkily, speaking for the first time. 'Or do you claim the rights of the church too? I wonder what the good Bishop Odo would say to that?' In an aside to Alyce, Gilbert murmured, 'Pray heaven you have got your facts right, lady.'

But Count Hubert had lost a little colour at the mention of the King's half-brother, who held great power and also the earldom of Kent. Alyce's sigh of relief was from the heart.

'Begone!' growled de Louches, rallying. 'This wench is of my household and this place is where she was hid, so here I shall do the punishing to show these serfs I am not one it is safe to displease.'

'But her crime, my lord?' insisted Roger. 'At least enlighten us on that point.'

'A stupid and unwilling servant who refused to do my bidding,' snarled the Count, goaded into reply. 'That is all you need to know.'

The girl raised her head, twisting her neck to look at Alyce. 'The charge is false, my lady. I worked as hard as any—as God is my witness—but what he asks is beyond all——'

'Enough!' roared de Louches, and the whip cracked, drowning the girl's words. Encouraged by their intervention, the crowd became restive and scraps of conversation rose.

'An honest worker she is——' 'Never unwilling to help anyone——' 'Not stupid either for she can read and write, they say——' 'How can he——?'

Alyce came to a decision. 'My lord Count!' She raised her clear voice above the murmurs. 'After this whipping, what do you intend?'

'To repeat it every day until she acknowledges me her master.'

'And then?'

'She will be of no further use to me. I shall sell her.'

'What a great deal of trouble you are putting yourself to, my lord,' Alyce said on a note of disinterest. 'And all for the sake of a disobedient girl. Why not put her up for sale at the start?' She gazed round innocently. 'I see not the King's sheriff nor yet the abbot's man. Should they not be represented in this matter? You have their consent to this act, of course?'

'A good point, lady,' whispered Gilbert, and waved his hand as if to brush a fly away from his forehead.

'Do I need consent,' Count Hubert began irritably, 'to deal with small matters concerning my own household?'

His head swivelled suddenly as he heard the jingle of harness, then his face suffused with red. He swung his heavy-jowled head from side to side and surveyed the ring of steel closing in on him with an expression of disbelief. Gaston, Roland and the twenty men-at-arms completely encircled him. The crowd had given way eagerly with a buzz of excitement, and the eight men of Count Hubert's force found themselves looking up into the helmeted, chain-mailed Beaumont escort, each man's hand resting on his sword-hilt.

'What is this?' roared the Count, but Alyce sensed that beneath his bluster there was real fear. She seized her advantage swiftly before he could recover.

'Why, Count, you must know that my father never allows me to leave the castle without escort. But no matter for that. You talked of selling the girl. Do you know, my lord, I have never been present at a public sale? Will you indulge my whim and allow me to witness the way of it? It will be most entertaining. How does one start?'

She clapped her hands, simulating childish glee, and forced a smile of excited anticipation.

Count Hubert's glance slid from Roger to Gilbert. Dark brows were raised expectantly, both faces half-smiling in mockery. He hesitated. God's bones, but they would pay for this!

'Come, Count,' urged Gilbert. 'Indulge the lady, for I know of your devotion to her. Have I not seen it at first hand?

Why do you hesitate? Do you wait for a dark corridor?' His laugh was low and sardonic.

De Louches knew he was beaten. The girl could be taken by superior force if he denied the request. His brows came down heavily. Rather than be humbled by de Boveney in front of this rabble, he must pretend to concede to the lady out of generosity. The ring of steel left no alternative.

'Very well, my lady. Because you ask this favour yourself, I will grant it, but remember and count it to my worth that I stayed my hand for you alone.'

He signed to his men to release the girl and began to roll down his sleeves. The arms of the fair girl fell to her sides, and Alyce saw the livid marks the thongs had left. As she rubbed her wrists the girl's eyes rested once, briefly and with scorn, upon the young soldier, then she turned and presented her back to him.

Alyce felt a moment of sympathy for the man. Her lover, perhaps? But the girl could not know, as Alyce did, that any attempt on his part to come to her aid would have been thwarted by one thrust of the dagger into his back.

The girl was led to the wooden platform outside the manor court. She stood proudly, her head thrown back, looking over the heads of the crowd towards Alyce. In spite of her proud stance, Alyce read fear and pleading in her eyes.

The Count swung himself on to a black stallion and sat with one hand on his hip. He seemed to have gained control of himself for his manner was jovial. His gaze passed insolently over the crowd. Who there could afford to bid for this girl? And who would dare?

What he had intended was done in a fit of passion, thoughtless perhaps, for the sheriff was out of the county and knew nothing of it, but none here would have objected, for he was the lord in these parts. Apart from the few who resided on glebe land—he should have remembered the village was in the Abbey holding—most were bound to the Manor and dare not, for their own sakes, raise objection. He cursed the unhappy accident of the Beaumont party chancing this way, but hid his rage, knowing that he could price her out of all reason. And the girl would still be his. Her punishment was not cancelled, but deferred until he had her back at the castle.

'Well?' he called loudly. 'Start the bidding.'

The crowd shuffled uneasily. One or two glanced at Alyce. No one spoke.

'Perhaps you crave to see the quality I am offering, more closely? Take off your clothes, girl. The bidding will be of more interest without those rags you clutch about you.'

The girl stood unmoving, her fingers buried in the torn bodice.

'With what you have left on her back,' Gaston observed from behind the Count, 'there hardly seems the necessity.' He was smiling in friendly fashion, but his eyes were cold. 'Leave the girl her modesty. Was it not her lack of industry you complained of? Or am I mistaken?'

'You are right,' said Count Hubert heartily. 'I thought to joke only, for the offers are slow. Come, my friends—make your bids. A strong wench for your kitchen or dairy. Who will start the bidding?'

The onlookers stared hopelessly at each other, for who could afford more than a few of their hoarded pennies? One tenant-farmer, secure on his glebe land, raised a hand. 'A shilling,' he offered tentatively. The crowd nodded approval.

The Count roared with laughter. 'A shilling—for a wench who will work from sun-up to sunset? You must think me wrong in the head, man. This servant is worth a hundred shillings or more.'

The farmer was silenced. The Count looked challengingly over the crowd and then at Alyce. 'You now see the way of it, my lady, but 'tis poor entertainment for you. Unless,' his eyes narrowed in suspicion, 'your noble escorts intend to join the bidding?'

'For what purpose, Count?' asked Roger. 'To have her polish armour and clean the stables?'

'You may find other talents in her,' suggested Count Hubert with a lewd smirk. 'But she will cost you dear.'

'I can put my money to better use, my lord, than buying favours from wenches.'

'My lady perhaps requires another servant?' asked Sir Hubert.

Alyce's lips parted. Why not? To save her from the Count, she would buy the girl herself. Out of the corner of her eye she caught a movement from Sir Gilbert. The heel of his boot jerked sharply into the belly of his horse, and the stallion jumped and danced sideways. Under cover of controlling his mount, Gilbert leaned towards her, a warning light in his eyes.

'Make no offer,' he muttered. 'Profess distaste for the whole affair.'

'But I can't leave her to him!' she whispered.

'We won't, but let him think it and feel safe. Trust me.'

What game was he playing? she wondered, but in this last hour she had come to respect his judgment. To trust him was the last thing she felt inclined to do, but if he had some scheme to free the girl, she must do as he asked. And Roger trusted his brother's instincts, so why should not she?

She raised her head. 'Another servant, my lord?' she echoed disdainfully. 'The castle is full of them. I swear they cost more to keep than is worth the trouble. If this is all the entertainment you are offering me, you may as well have kept your generosity to yourself and left the girl on the whipping-post. I count this no special favour to me!'

The Count's eyes gleamed in satisfaction. 'Perhaps Sir Gilbert, then——?' He must make sure that he had no opponents but this parcel of stupid peasants.

'My interest is even less, Count,' remarked Gilbert, his voice a cutting edge, 'so don't waste your time, lest I suspect that even for a hundred shillings you would not part with her for reasons of your own.'

'You wrong me, Sir Knight. Could any worthy person here come forward with that amount, I would hand her over right gladly.' He stared round earnestly. 'Come, my friends, your silence insults our noble visitors. The first offer of a hundred shillings from one of you wins this wench, by my oath.'

No one raised his voice. The Count's eyes slid over the girl. In less than an hour she would realise the cost of her defiance. That soft white body would lie in his bed, the choice hers —unmarked or beaten into submission. Either way he would win. He was full of impatience to put an end to this farce and taste the joys of mastery.

With his eyes still on the shrinking girl he began, 'In that case, my friends, I have no alternative but——'

Sir Gilbert flashed Alyce a quick look. His smile was cruel. 'We have him! Make your bid.'

Alyce's heart leaped in exultation. Her voice rang out imperiously. 'On my oath then, lord Count, I will meet your demand. I will take the girl, for my dear Edith grows a little slow and needs a girl to fetch and carry.'

The Count came out of his lewd contemplation with a start. He stared, his eyes narrowing. A vein stood out thickly on his forehead. God's teeth! Was he to be denied, then?

''Twas but a figure I drew out of the air. She is worth more. Did I not own her, I would bid two hundred myself.'

'But you do own her, my lord,' said Sir Gilbert reasonably, 'so that argument is beside the point. You swore to accept the first offer of a hundred shillings. My Lady Alyce has made that offer.' He looked round at the villagers. 'Is it a fair offer, my friends?'

There was a roar of approval and a stamping of feet.

'I will not sell her,' returned the Count on a shout, his face scarlet with passion. 'I withdraw her. She is worth five hundred, I tell you.'

'You swore an oath, Count. Is it so worthless that you go back on it and now seek to raise her price?' Gilbert's voice cut through the noise like the point of a dagger, sharp, probing, twisting hard into the vitals of the sweating man. The Count's eyes were fixed on him with the angry stare of an outraged bull denied the freedom of the farmyard. The crowd quietened, scenting that this was not the end of the spectacle they were enjoying.

'You know, brother,' said Roger, turning in his saddle, 'it seems the good Count is loath to part with this treasure.' His voice was light and carried clearly across the market square. 'Five hundred shillings for a disobedient servant! He must be excessively attached to her, and yet he planned to whip her. I scent a mystery here. Perhaps the girl has knowledge of a Saxon hoard of buried jewels, and the Count covets this hidden fortune.'

'Or could it be,' replied Gilbert in a voice that carried equally well but held an undercurrent of grim humour, 'that what the Count covets is a treasure not of the past, but of the present, and the girl has sole charge of that and desires not to relinquish it.'

Alyce glanced uncertainly from one to the other. They spoke in riddles, and yet it made sense to one of the watching men. The Count stirred uneasily and forced a laugh.

'No mystery, good sirs. I got carried away in the heat of the moment. I grew fond of the wench for all her disobedience. Let us forget the matter. Go on your way and I will revoke her punishment and take her back to my castle.'

'A little too late for that, my lord. She now belongs to my Lady Alyce.'

Roger grinned. 'For my part, Gil, I have no objection to discovering the true worth of this girl, for she is obviously a pearl above price to my lord Count.'

'And a good joke to share with the King,' added Gilbert. 'I doubt he ever heard of a serving wench on sale for five hundred shillings.'

'Have done,' said Count Hubert, glowering. 'I grow tired of this matter. Take the slut, my lady, and good riddance.'

'Thank you, my lord. You may send your steward to the castle for payment.' She beckoned to the girl who moved quickly towards her, Gaston and Roland behind.

'I'll take her up, my lady,' offered Gaston, and Alyce smilingly accepted his offer. The crowd broke up, many warm glances thrown in their direction. Merchants hurried back to their stalls and voices rose as the market place resumed its usual activity. Alyce thought of the young soldier and her glance searched for him. He stood alone now, but his eyes were fixed not on the girl but on Alyce. Relief and gratitude glowed on his face. He made no move towards the girl, now perched pillion behind Gaston. Alyce smiled at him, determined to explain to the girl the reason behind the apparent desertion of her lover.

As she wheeled her horse to follow Roger, Count Hubert had moved, thrusting his stallion through the thinning crowd. He sidled his horse close to hers, and she looked with repulsion into his sweating face.

'I will expect payment for this, my lady.'

She looked at him coldly. 'Naturally, Lord Count. I have already said that you may send your steward to the castle.'

'The money is nothing.' He dismissed it with a contemptuous snap of the fingers. 'Her worth was above money.'

'So I gathered, but in what way, my lord?'

What an innocent she was! he thought. And how he would enjoy the teaching of her! His smile was amused, but the glance that drifted over her was tinged with some secret knowledge that chilled her blood.

His voice was low, almost caressing. 'One day you will learn, my lady, and that will be my payment.'

CHAPTER FIVE

'Come, Lady Alyce,' Roger spoke from her side. 'The Count has run out of entertainment, so there is nothing more to delay our ride.' He had swung back on realising Alyce's interception by Count Hubert, and was curious to know why she had grown pale.

She looked at him gratefully and turned her palfrey, trying to dismiss the cold chill caused by Count Hubert's words. What they meant she could not imagine, but the feeling that he planned something in revenge stayed with her.

They rode away from the now bustling hamlet. The villagers cheered and waved their caps as the party progressed down the beaten earth track. The sullen air was gone; Lady Alyce had saved the girl as they had known she would. The peasant girls smiled shyly at the knights and men-at-arms and looked with awe at the stern-faced knight who had driven the lord Count into a frenzy of rage, then lashed him with a tongue as sharp as the jewelled dagger he carried. He had a dangerous look about him, that one, but he was with the Lady Alyce so they smiled on him too, for he had bested the hated Count.

The other knight, so like the stern-faced one they must be brothers, was smiling in return, his gaze so merry and bold they liked him the best of all the knights. To have a lord like that instead of the Count would make their duties at the castle a pleasure. And none would end at the whipping-post as the girl, Meg, had. They waved to her too as she clung to the waist of the pleasant-faced knight with her corn-coloured hair streaming behind. She would be safe with the Lady Alyce, as long as she kept her distance from the village.

Once out on to the common with the village far behind, there was an air of gaiety about the party. Even the men-at-arms, while not forgetting their duties as escort, grinned at each other, passing low-voiced comments on the discomfiture of the Count. Most of them had some friend or relative working on de Louches land, and it gave them pleasure to witness the Count so thwarted. Their respect for the de Boveneys had risen, too. Anyone who could stand against such a man and win the day was to be admired.

Alyce had ridden in silence so far, seeking to dispel the feeling of unease that still clung to her. Roger reached over and touched her hand.

'You are quiet, my lady. Are you not glad we succeeded in freeing the girl?'

'Of course I am glad, but at what cost, I wonder?'

Riding on her other side, Gilbert glanced at her still pale face. 'But something troubles you. Do you think Count Hubert will be doubly cruel to those who remain behind?'

'Perhaps, but I feel the matter is far from ended. From the look on his face and the way he smiled as we left, I fear he has some scheme to avenge this defeat. Look to yourselves, messires, for those whom the Count hates go in peril of their lives.'

Roger's fingers closed comfortingly over her hand. 'We leave in a few days, my lady, so there is little he can do in that time. But tell me, what were those last words of his to you? He cut through that crowd so quickly I was not aware of his intention. Did he dare to threaten you?'

'No, but his remark was strange. He spoke as if I had not already invited him to send over his steward for payment.'

Roger frowned. 'What else, my lady?'

'Nothing really, except to repeat his remark about the girl's worth being above money.'

Still frowning, Roger glanced at his brother. 'What does that devil's spawn have in mind, do you suppose?'

'He was so reluctant to part with the girl, I wonder if he plans to snatch her back. After the King has left, of course. He would dare nothing before.'

Alyce's brow cleared. 'That must be it. I will warn the girl to stay within sight of the castle at all times, although she appears intelligent enough to know that without being told. After her experience she will not put herself within Count Hubert's reach again.' She shuddered. 'He really *is* a pig.'

A glance at Gilbert's suddenly raised brows reminded her of that late meeting in the corridor, and she laughed. 'But a wild boar, ugly and hairy, not like the ones in our sty. And now let us talk of something pleasant. Does the King mean to take part in the tournament tomorrow?'

'I doubt it, my lady. He was a great one for the contests in his younger days, I understand, but there is too much at stake for him now to risk life and limb on the jousting field.'

'I am so looking forward to it,' Alyce said, favouring each knight with a glowing glance and her black hair swung about as she looked from one to the other. Her skin was peach-like in the sunshine, delicately tinted with pink, and the deep blue velvet of her riding outfit matched the veil fluttering behind. Her slim figure swayed with the motion of the palfrey and her gloved hands were elegant on the reins.

Roger watched her, smiling, and she veiled her eyes with lashes that swept her cheeks as she read the desire in his gaze. Was this feeling of power the same as the one Queen Matilda knew? How she longed to return his look, but it was too soon. The King would not as yet have spoken to her father, but before the visit ended he would have done so. By the time the court was due to leave and she had received approval from both the King and her father, only then could she surrender to Roger's arms and declare her love for him.

She gazed straight ahead, recalling his kiss and the gentle words of love. Could any royal visit ever have such a wonderful ending as this?

The castle was reached and she left the knights in the bailey. The girl she took with her to her room. Edith looked up, startled, as they entered. She eyed the girl in silence for a moment, then recognition came slowly.

'Why, it is Margaret, daughter of Oswald the carpenter who died last year.' Alarm crossed her face. 'What do you here, child? You are bound to the manor of the Lord de Louches——'

'No longer, dear Edith,' said Alyce, 'for I have bought her from him. Do you know, she was tied to the whipping-post when we chanced upon the scene! How glad I am that you mentioned 'twas market day in the village. We should not have been there otherwise.'

The girl fell to her knees, her hands clasping Alyce's. 'I thank God and your kindness, my lady, for that chance. Had you not been there——' Her voice broke, and tears fell on Alyce's fingers.

'The whipping-post!' Edith was aghast. 'What thing had you done to deserve such fate?'

The girl raised her eyes and said bitterly. 'It takes little to rouse the lord Count to anger, but usually the beating is done in his castle where none can see. I ran away and hid in the village, but he found me.'

'And that was his mistake,' said Alyce. 'Had he dragged you back to his castle none would have known, but his anger was such that he could not wait to punish you.'

'But what——?' began Edith.

Alyce interrupted quickly as the girl swayed. 'Never mind now, Edith. Help her to the couch before she faints. Call Ranulf and tell him to bring food. She is weak and perhaps has eaten nothing all day. And then find her something to wear—her dress is ripped beyond hope.'

'Yes, my lady,' Edith fled to the door and Alyce heard her voice calling for Ranulf as she gazed down on the girl. The eyes opened and the girl tried to pull herself to her feet.

'Lie still,' ordered Alyce.

'But in your presence, my lady——'

'You will do as I bid,' she smiled. 'Or I shall be angry. But never fear that any in the service of the Beaumonts are treated harshly. My lord father is a kind man and no one has ever been whipped here. You are called Margaret, I believe?'

'Yes, my lady, but mostly I am known as Meg.'

'Would you like to stay here and be my maidservant under Edith, or do you prefer some other position?'

'Whatever my lady commands. There is nothing I will not do for you. If you wish me to tend pigs I will do it gladly out of eternal gratitude.'

'Good heavens, Meg! We have boys to do that. Can you sew?'

'Yes, my lady, for I was taught by the nuns but put in the kitchens by my lord Count. The old women only were allowed to mend and sew, after they had worn out their strength on kitchen work or with the attentions of the men-at-arms.'

Alyce hesitated, then asked slowly and a little uncertainly, 'Are you saying that the men-at-arms had the freedom of the kitchen girls? Do I understand you correctly?'

'You do, my lady.' The girl's voice was low. 'His service attracts only the scum of the shire, those whose ways are akin to his.'

'But what of the girls? Did they not object to such treatment?'

Meg's mouth twisted. 'Most were from the gutters themselves.' Her eyes smouldered resentfully. 'But I was not a tavern wench, and fought them with whatever came to hand until they left me alone.'

'Was that the reason for the whipping?'

'No, my lady, for none dared touch me after the Count came across me one day. He forbade his men to lay a finger on me and I took it for kindness, for I was young and inexperienced.'

'It doesn't sound like him to be kind without reason.'

'He had good reason, as I found out later from odd remarks. I was being reserved for his pleasure.' She looked down and her cheeks reddened. 'He knew I was untouched.'

Alyce's senses reeled. 'He would have forced you?' she stammered, remembering her own experience with the Count. She had not really believed his words that night, thinking him far gone in wine, but now she wondered. Even a nobly-born girl under her own roof? Was it possible?

Her mind revolted. What had Sir Gilbert said that night? Something about those who had no protection, like the peasants on de Louches land. She thought suddenly of the young soldier in the market square.

'Did no one help you?'

Meg's eyes went hard. 'I thought there was one, but he proved false.'

'One of the men-at-arms?'

'Yes, my lady. He treated me kindly and with affection. He said he hated the Count but was bound in his service for the year. We grew fond of each other and decided to marry—in that way I could have left the castle.'

'What happened?'

'We asked permission of the Count as was proper, and he agreed most heartily. We could be married immediately by his chaplain, he said, and he would arrange everything. We were married this morning, my lady, and I was so happy. I kissed the Count's hand and told him I should ever be grateful for his kindness. I could hardly believe it, he even took wine with us, and I began to think that what was said of him was untrue.'

'We drank our wine in his own room from silver goblets. A most beautiful room with tapestries on the walls, fur rugs and gold hangings over the bed. He sent my new husband to saddle the horse and then gave me more wine. And then—then I learned why I was being so honoured.'

Her lips curled in disgust. 'He spoke some foreign words—French, I think—but I did not understand him. He said it was the custom—the right of the lord—to claim the first night.'

'God's bones!' breathed Alyce, unconsciously voicing a favourite oath of her father's. 'The *droit du Seigneur*! I thought that custom was dead.'

'I know nothing of that, my lady, but those were the words he used. I was simple-minded enough to think the Count had put aside his own intentions for me, but my marriage only brought forward the time of it.'

They were disturbed by the entrance of Ranulf, bearing a bowl of thick vegetable soup and a roll of bread.

'Eat now, Meg,' said Alyce, and turned towards the window. She gripped the stone sill and gazed unseeingly across the countryside.

What could she do? Dare she speak to the King? Perhaps she was simple-minded too, and the 'right of the lord' was not so uncommon as she had supposed. Perhaps all lords claimed the new bride as a bedmate before allowing her to return to her husband, no longer a virgin. If only she was older and knew more of the world, but at this moment she dared not speak of it to anyone for fear they would admit it and laugh her to scorn.

She turned back to Meg who was finishing her soup. Her face had gained a little colour, and she looked up gratefully at Alyce.

'But you escaped, Meg. You managed to run away and hide in the village.'

Meg nodded. 'The Count was angry and locked me in his room when I begged to be released. He said had I been willing to return his kindness, I might have left within the hour, but my defiance made him determined to have me stay the whole night. I was so desperate to escape that I climbed from the window and crawled along a ledge. I clung to a buttress for hours, it seemed, until there was no one about, then I threw myself into the moat.

'I expected to kill myself but when I came to the surface I was near the far side. Somehow I climbed out, then I ran until I reached a barn where I hid under the straw while my clothes dried. I thought to wait until dark and escape, but the Count had discovered I'd gone. They came searching and found me.'

'But your husband, Meg? What of him?'

'Husband? I have no husband! Save a tame dog who would stand by and watch the Count do as he wished.' Her face was like stone, her blue eyes hard.

Alyce knelt impulsively beside her couch. 'Nay, Meg, you are wrong. One move towards you and he would have been dead on the spot. Did you not see how closely hemmed in he was?'

Meg frowned. 'I saw the sergeant-at-arms behind him, but——' Her gaze rose. 'How could you know, my lady, of my husband?'

'I saw much more than you think. The man behind held a dagger to his back. It flashed in the sun for an instant and I knew that the man—your lover, I thought—was held against his will. Don't judge him so harshly, Meg. What could he do against such odds? No doubt he was held in confinement by the Count's orders the moment he set foot in the stables.'

Meg nodded, her eyes softening. Tears welled up and ran unheeded down her cheeks. 'But when I was freed, he never approached me.' She looked up in bewilderment.

Alyce patted her shoulder. 'He was being wise for your sake. I saw his face. No man showed such joy and relief as he did. You were safe—but he is still tied to the Count, remember. What could he have done had he approached you but draw the Count's rage on to himself? He showed wisdom there. He has not deserted you, I am convinced of that. Ah, here is Edith.' She rose to her feet. 'Go with her now and she will show you where the girls sleep. Rest tonight and come to me tomorrow, and we will decide on your duties.'

'My lady—how can I ever thank you?'

'You can show me how well the nuns taught you to sew,' Alyce replied, smiling. 'Go now with Edith.'

Meg curtsied, her face aglow with gratitude, and left the room. Alyce paced the floor awhile, dwelling on the possibility of an attempt by the Count to retrieve the girl. She was in no doubt that he would continue to visit her father in spite of the humiliation of the day—but after the King's departure, she judged. Earl Robert was not a man to see evil in any who had fought alongside the King, and he would dismiss the girl's account as wild kitchen talk. Even her own encounter with de Louches could be laughed off as a childish imagining. Oh, yes, Count Hubert's ready tongue had only to claim that all he intended was to bestow a bedtime kiss on his friend's beloved child and her father would be convinced. Although she could not herself be excused each time the Count called, she was determined that Meg should be under guard for the duration of his visits.

The guests at the evening meal that night were fewer. The neighbouring lords had returned to their own estates, leaving only the King's party. William was in good humour, his successful hunt putting him in high spirits. The tables were set closer so that all could converse together, and Alyce was delighted to find Roger beside her. Across from the King sat Sir Gilbert.

All the men wore the evening dress of an ankle-length tunic, belted at the waist and decorated at neck, sleeve-edges and hem to suit their own tastes. To give freedom of movement, the long skirts were split at each side up to the knee, revealing shorter under-tunics and jewelled leather boots.

The King, of course, was the most richly dressed man present, his tunic embroidered in gold thread and set with pearls, a narrow circlet of gold on his brow. By stern contrast, Sir Gilbert's tunic was black with little decoration anywhere. His only jewel was a heavy gold signet ring, engraved with the de Boveney arms. With his grave, unsmiling eyes on the King, he had a stark quality about him. Did he never laugh, just for the sheer joy of living? Alyce wondered.

Then she turned towards Roger, gay in a bronze-coloured tunic, decorated with blue geometric designs, over which hung a chain of gold links. He had been watching as her eyes rested on Gilbert.

'Well, my lady?' he asked. 'What is your summing-up? A touch sombre, wouldn't you say?' His eyes laughed at her confusion. 'I warned him that someone might think he had come to deliver a funeral oration, but he told me in no uncertain manner to go and soak my head—that he had no wish to appear like a King's fool or travelling minstrel, he would leave that to me.' He grinned so infectiously that Alyce laughed.

'How very ungenerous of him! I think you look most elegant. Your brother reminds me of a raven, one that sits, watchful and a little sinister, on the castle ramparts. Does he never wear jewels?'

'None, apart from the ring. It is one of a pair our father had made for us. I rarely wear mine because of the weight of it, but Gil is never parted from his.'

The King, who had been talking of the speed and success of Earl Robert's hawks, asked suddenly if the Lady Alyce's party had enjoyed their excursion in the lowlands. Sir Gilbert's eyes glinted and he smiled slightly.

'Indeed, Sire, for my part I took great pleasure from it. I've enjoyed nothing so well for many a day.'

'I am glad you were able to provide entertainment, my

lady,' remarked the King approvingly. 'Sir Gilbert is no easy man to please. What was it you provided?'

With a mind suddenly blank, Alyce sought desperately for something to say. Her glance met Gilbert's and a gleam of mockery showed in his dark eyes as her confusion mounted.

'To be fair, Sire,' he went on smoothly, his gaze returning to the King, 'the entertainment was already under way when we arrived, and we were able to witness its happy conclusion. There was indeed a little excitement, for it was market day, as my lady had foretold.'

'Ah, I see. With juggling and bear-baiting, I suppose?'

Gilbert paused. He looked down at his plate, then said on a musing note, 'A little of both now I think on it, but on a small scale only. Nothing of any great consequence but it pleased the villagers.'

Someone gave a choke of laughter. Alyce dragged her fascinated gaze from Sir Gilbert and observed Roland, grinning all over his face and beating Gaston on the back.

'Your pardon, Sire,' gasped Sir Gaston as soon as he was able to speak. 'A crust of bread lodged in my throat when de Boveney spoke of the bear-baiting.' His eyes met Gilbert's, then he looked away hastily, trying to control his expression.

Beside her, Roger gave a low chuckle. 'A fair description of the entertainment, wouldn't you say, my lady?'

'Your brother has a smooth tongue,' Alyce remarked dryly, stung by Sir Gilbert's mocking glance. 'Does he never want for words?'

'It is on occasions a generous tongue,' Roger said quietly.

Was there a hint of reproof in his voice? Alyce stared at him. 'What does that mean, sir?'

Roger eyed her with a gentle look. 'Surely you realise his intervention saved you from the King's more searching questions? You were taken by surprise. How would you have replied? With the truth, and have the King support de Louches?'

Alyce was silent for a moment. 'You are right,' she said at last. 'And I owe your brother an apology. I could not have passed it off in that way, and the King would have suspected something amiss by my manner.'

Roger squeezed her hand reassuringly. 'Don't look so downcast, my lady. You are young yet. Given time, your tongue will be as versatile as any court lady's. But pray you, do not hurry that moment, for I much prefer your sweetness now. You are like a rosebud, compared with the overblown blossoms of our court.'

'Barely a bud, I would guess to your brother, but then I suppose he prefers the blossoms you speak of.'

''Tis true he could take his pick of them, for they find his coolness a challenge, but he rarely takes up that challenge save carelessly, and none has yet entrapped and bound him to her side with perfumed tendrils.' He laughed softly. 'Our lord father has given up filling the house with worthy maidens, beauties and heiresses alike. Gil will make his own choice and in his own time.'

'Perhaps like the King he will love only once. But my sympathy lies with the girl his choice will fall upon.'

'Why so, Alyce?'

'Is it not true that William took a whip to the Lady Matilda when she stood against him before their marriage?'

'That is the story, yes, and I believe it to be true. But she loved him for all that.'

'She must have done so to suffer such painful handling and still wed him. Your brother has similar qualities to the King's. I wonder if he will deal as hardly with the one he chooses?'

'The King, when Duke of Normandy, had a hard upbringing, Alyce. He had no time or talent for gentle courtship—he was too busy holding his Duchy together. Times are different now. Gil may be like him in some respects, but I've never known him ill-treat a woman.'

'Have you ever known him in love?'

LADY OF STARLIGHT 65

'Never! But why talk of Gil? I would much rather talk of us.'

'Us? In what way, sir?' Her lashes swept down, hiding the glow in her eyes.

'You must know my feelings for you, Alyce. Can I hope that you may return them? Will you not give me your answer tonight—on the battlements?'

'I think you know it already, sir,' she said on a half-laugh. 'And so does——'

There was a roar of laughter from the main body of the hall. Alyce turned, to hear the King say, 'So—we will put that boast to the test, Sir Knight.' He stared round the company, his grey eyes alight with challenge. 'Let us put all here to the test and discover a champion. With your permission, Earl Robert, we will clear the hall and every man shall be allotted an opponent. The last to remain on his feet will receive this ruby ring from my hand. Do you all accept?'

There was a burst of applause and Alyce turned, bewildered, to Roger. His smile was rueful.

'The King is in jovial mood. He means us to wrestle with each other. It used to be a favourite sport of his.'

Alyce sighed with relief. 'For a moment I suspected he meant you to fight with swords when he spoke of the last man on his feet.'

Roger smiled. 'I am afraid we must all obey him in this, so the meeting I hoped for tonight must be delayed. Can you forgive me? I thought to be looking at the stars in your company, but now it seems I must wrestle for the King's pleasure when all I desire is to hold you in my arms.'

'You cannot disobey a royal command,' Alyce said, her heart heavy with disappointment.

'I wish I could slip away but the King will count heads. He has the sight of a hawk.'

'You must not try, Roger,' she protested softly. 'There are other nights, and the stars will still be there.'

CHAPTER SIX

SHORTLY afterwards Alyce withdrew from the great hall. She had no wish to watch and none would expect it, for the men were to be stripped to the waist and bare-footed. In the heat of excitement too, their language might not be suitable for her ears.

On reaching her room she found the girl waiting. 'Why, Meg!' she exclaimed, 'I thought you would be fast asleep by now. Why do you wait, and where is Edith?'

'Forgive me, my lady, but Edith was weary so I told her I would be honoured to help you to bed. Did I do wrong?' She raised her eyes half-fearfully.

'Of course not, but surely you are weary yourself after all that has happened today?'

'I am strong, my lady, and must do all in my power to serve you and be worthy of your condescension.'

Alyce smiled. 'I did little, Meg, and without the knights beside me could have done nothing. It is they you should thank.'

'I do, my lady, with all my heart, and if you will allow me to take Edith's pallet, I would sleep here in your chamber tonight.'

'You may if you wish it, but you have nothing to fear from any of our men-at-arms. My father allows no behaviour of that sort within the castle.' She could understand the girl's nervousness and was prepared to make allowances for it. 'When you have become used to us here, you will be quite free from worry and none will molest you. I need not add a warning about wandering too near the village, need I?'

A vehement shake of the corn-coloured hair was sufficient answer.

Later, as Alyce lay in bed, the sounds of revelry, distant but sustained, reached her. The starlight glimmered through the arched window of her chamber and she reflected sadly on the joy she had missed.

But the visit was not yet over. Two nights remained. Two nights during which she could stand shoulder to shoulder with Roger on the battlements, with the breeze in her hair and the sweet scent of herbs drifting upwards. And Roger would take her hands in his and kiss her with more passion than was possible in the openness of the stables. A secret plighting of their troth, she thought with a delicious shiver running through her. And with the King's promise—she yawned—what could be simpler than an announcement on the last night of their visit?

Her eyelids drooped. The distant hum from the great hall flowed through her drifting mind, rising and falling like the chanting of angel choirs.

She woke to full daylight with the joy still in her. There was much to do, for the tournament was to start as soon as they had eaten. She glanced from her window. The sky was clear with merely a handful of tiny clouds floating high and white under the azure dome. Sunlight beat down, and from the direction of the meadow beyond the bailey she caught the sound of hammering.

Circular marquees, striped red and blue, were in place, the breeze rippling their sides and scalloped fringes of white that encircled them at roof height. Each roof rose to a point and on each point fluttered an ensign embroidered with the emblem of a noble house. Long before the tournament began, the squires and armourers would gather to prepare the armour and weapons for their knights. Helmets and shields polished to brilliance, lances checked for faults and horses groomed and brushed until their coats shone with like brilliance.

She came out of her absorption to hear the thunder of hooves on the drawbridge. The neighbouring lords with their lady wives had all been invited to return for the tournament. The King's champion was due, in addition: Alyce had never seen him but he was reputed to be unbeatable and lacked no challengers for his honoured position.

Meg came in with hot water, followed by Edith carrying a tray of food. The gown Alyce planned to wear was of amber silk, the sleeves long and flowing, banded about with rich embroidery to match the neckline. Her head-veil was of gold silk, secured by a plaited band of gold thread, and she wore her tasselled girdle.

As Edith slipped on the soft leather heel-less shoes, Meg held the silver mirror before Alyce, who regarded herself critically. She was not displeased. The amber silk was barely lighter than her own eye-colour and the material followed the curves of her figure before falling with satisfying grace to her ankles. She was slender but shapely, and her waist could be spanned by two hands. The hot summer had tinted her skin with a delicate sheen, highlighting the glow of her amber eyes.

'My lady looks beautiful,' Meg breathed ecstatically. 'Do you not think so, Edith?'

Edith looked Alyce up and down. 'A fair enough sight,' she admitted, and Alyce smiled, for Edith could not quite hide the pride in her eyes as she placed the silk-lined mantle over her mistress's shoulders and secured it with a jewelled brooch on the right shoulder.

Ranulf came pounding along the passageway to tell her that Earl Robert awaited her with His Majesty. He had got over his fright of yesterday, but was still in great awe of the King. She asked him who had arrived a short while before at the gatehouse.

'Sir Lionel d'Eston, my lady, the King's champion. They

say that no man has yet beaten him in the lists, though many have tried. 'Twill be great sport watching the knights endeavour to unseat him before the King.'

Ranulf fell behind as they came into the hall. The King stood amongst his nobles, magnificent in his purple tunic with the circlet of gold on his brow. Beside him stood her father, tall, grey-haired and in his usual dark colours.

Alyce made her curtsy to the King and received a warm embrace from her father, then allowed her gaze to wander over the assembly as she joined the ladies, bright and glittering like exotic birds in plumage of every colour. There was a movement from the hall to the bailey and Alyce caught her father's beckoning gesture.

The King turned. 'Come, my lady. Let de Boveney have the honour of escorting you to the field.' He laughed. 'Earl Robert and I will escort ourselves.'

Alyce looked up eagerly as Gilbert bowed and offered her his arm. She tried to hide her disappointment, for he was looking at her quizzically.

'The King commands, lady. We must obey. I know this is not to your liking, so I suggest we declare a truce.'

She regarded him suspiciously. 'On what terms?'

He laughed. 'No terms, my lady, unless you impose them. Just a cessation of hostilities while we are in the King's sight. After the tournament you are free to take up arms again. For your information, Roger is already in the marquee, impatient for the bouts to start so that you may admire his white Arab stallion. He bids me tell you he means to challenge Sir Lionel d'Eston.'

As her eyes widened, he went on dryly, 'Of course he hopes you will not only admire the Arab.'

She caught the glint of sardonic humour in his eye and bit back a sharp retort. Whether she liked it or not, she must show no public discourtesy to this man. Whatever his personal feelings on being commanded to escort her, he was prepared to do it with the courtesy due to her rank and the deference due to her sex. His next remark caught her off-balance.

'May I say, my lady, that your beauty is outstanding today? That amber silk was an inspired choice. It shows your eyes to their best advantage and the gown itself gives me cause to admit I was wrong in my assessment.'

For a moment she was speechless, staring at him. Was this a deliberate move to throw her into confusion? Well, two could play that game! A tiny smile quivered on her lips.

'Why, thank you, Sir Gilbert,' she said demurely, 'I do believe that is the first compliment you have paid me in three days. With your vast experience of female charms, I am honoured to think my poor display is worthy of such gallantry. I was just getting used to your curt orders and rough treatment too! I am overwhelmed by your condescension to one so——' She paused, her lashes sweeping her cheeks. 'So young. Confess it for the truth, Sir Gilbert. You see me no other way.' Her gaze rose in challenge.

His eyes had narrowed. His regard was strangely intent, deepening the slight furrow on his brow. A tiny spark glowed for an instant in the depths of his eyes, then was gone. '*Mea culpa*,' he said smoothly. 'I stand accused of an obtuseness amounting to gross discourtesy. My first impression was heightened on the night of our encounter with de Louches. Against him you appeared as tiny and fragile as the child I took you for. But on one point, my lady, I was certainly not mistaken, as you proved a little later.'

'And what was that, sir?' She eyed him warily, suddenly tense.

'Your spirit. You would even fight fate alone with the greatest ferocity at your command, unless it had first rendered you senseless or disabled.'

'Well, naturally. If I am to be raped, then I demand some choice in the manner of its accomplishment.'

He stared at her for a second in stunned silence, then his lips quivered and his eyes filled with laughter. In that second she realised the illogicality of her remark, and her own eyes lit with merriment.

'How stupid,' she gasped unsteadily. 'I think you must reverse your opinion once more, Sir Gilbert, if indeed you had ever changed it.'

For answer he took her hand and placed it in the crook of his elbow, and they began a slow stroll across the clipped grass towards the meadow.

'No, my lady. Most definitely not.' His smile held, not the mockery she expected, but a look of genuine enjoyment. 'I find your tongue refreshingly different. If you ever come to court, I hope you will not become like the rest, filled with gossip and intrigue, changing their lovers as often as their gowns.'

'My father is not a courtier, and as we have no queen, that event is hardly likely. Is court life not then to your taste, Sir Gilbert?' she asked, thinking of Roger's remarks on his brother's success with the ladies.

'The headiest fragrance grows stale after a time, and one seeks a breath of fresh air. But the older one gets, the harder it becomes to find.'

'But once you find it, will you be content? Or will the accustomed fragrance of the court draw you back?'

'When I find what I seek—if such thing is possible, and I doubt it—then nothing will draw me back save the command of the King.'

Did he speak of love, she wondered? But what kind of a woman could hold this man, so like the King? Not a court lady, she supposed from Roger's talk, but a woman perhaps like the Lady Matilda. A woman of strong will, but feminine enough to capture his heart. He would scorn a submissive one but pursue an elusive spirit and glory in the chase of one strong enough to defy him.

Perhaps it was that kind of ruthlessness that drew the women to him. But the woman must be sure of her own heart first, for Sir Gilbert, like the King, would hold fast.

For some reason Alyce felt a disinclination to continue in this vein. Whatever he sought—or had lost—she was reluctant to appear prying, in case he should revert to his usual hard manner.

'Tell me of the King, Sir Gilbert. Is it true he plans a great land survey?'

'Quite true. It has just begun and already the people have a name for it. They call it Domesday.'

He smiled at her startled, questioning look. 'I imagine because there is no escape from the King's Commissioners, and all must be revealed as it will be on the day of judgment.'

'Tell me of it, please.'

'It has been in his mind for some time, so he called his council together at Gloucester to deliberate on the method of achieving this great task. He aims to know how much land is in each shire and how it is peopled, so his Commissioners are travelling the country recording each acre of land and all the livestock thereon. It must be recorded, too, who holds each manor now and who held it in King Edward's day. Even Abbots and Earls cannot avoid replying to the Commissioners.' Gilbert smiled. 'It will be so well done, rumour has it, that no pig, however small, will escape notice.'

'It sounds most thorough, but what is the purpose of this survey?'

'It is to be a permanent record of the amount of land belonging to each landholder in the kingdom. The King desires to know how much the Crown holds and what dues are lawfully his from each shire. It will be the first time such records of land and people have been kept.'

'I begin to see the point of it,' Alyce remarked. 'This information, truthfully recorded, will be of the utmost value to His Majesty, apart from the knowledge it contains of the land and population.'

'Yes, my lady?' Gilbert's sideways glance was speculative. 'And what would you guess is the point of it?'

'It will be used for the purpose of taxation. None can avoid that imposition if it is written in this—this Domesday book that his land is worth the amount stated.'

Gilbert's eyebrows rose. 'A shrewd comment, lady. With every mill, fishpond, wood and pasture noted, the Commissioners will know to the penny how much every man is worth.'

''Tis the King who is shrewd, sir.'

'Doubly true, my lady,' he laughed softly. 'For there is a second body to check the findings of the first. Our King leaves nothing to chance. Men may speak harshly of him, but he will knit this realm together under the crown as no monarch ever did. It is a foundation on which to build truth and justice for all men. Who can argue with that?'

'You admire him greatly, do you not?'

'There is some quality about him that would call me to his side, even were I not pledged to him as a knight.'

'I have heard him described as a dread King, proud and arrogant.'

'He is described truly. As a young Duke, he scorned those who decried his low birth. He was proud of his sire's heritage and arrogant in reply by always inscribing beneath his signature, for all to see, *cognomine Bastardus*.'

'That took courage.'

'Something he is not short of, my lady. And perhaps for that reason only, my sword is against any who seek his downfall, noble or commoner, man or woman.'

'Woman, Sir Gilbert? Could a woman raise arms against the King?'

'You think a woman has no weapons?' he asked, smiling down at her. 'She bears arms enough to send a man reeling. An attack on the senses can weaken a man's will to fight.'

'But the King is no untried boy. He must have known many women, yet none has swayed him from his purpose.'

'William had his Matilda. But I was thinking of lesser men, those who were once hungry to serve him but now, if danger threatens, will be reluctant to leave their rich holdings and the arms of their mistresses.'

'That is unfair, Sir Gilbert. Why should their oaths prove less strong than yours? For you yourself must have known many——' She stopped, aghast, her eyes flashing upwards. 'Forgive me——'

To her intense relief he was smiling. 'A few, my lady, as any normal man has. But I have discovered an immunity to such poison. I cannot be unmanned for I have no heart—or so I have been told many times.'

'I can well understand it, Sir Gilbert, for I have thought that myself, yet I believe we misjudge you a little.'

His brows rose in surprise. 'A little is progress indeed coming from you, my lady. What can I have done to earn such approbation?'

Alyce stared into the dark eyes, determined to ignore what she took to be a smile of mockery. 'You may think it nothing, sir, but to the girl you saved from a whipping it meant a great deal. Perhaps you acted from hatred of de Louches, but that does not apply to last night.'

'Last night? I can recall nothing to my credit.'

'During dinner, when the King asked what entertainment I had provided, my mind emptied itself of all the wits I possess.'

'Oh, that! I admit I saw your confusion and thought it best to intervene.'

'For a moment your look seemed to mock my confusion, but you took the King's attention away, and for that I am in your debt, Sir Gilbert.'

By this time they had reached the stands. The King was in the place of honour beneath a crimson silk canopy on which the lions of England rippled golden in the sun.

Gilbert halted and looked down into the shining face of the slender girl by his side. Something stirred in his heart, but he pushed aside the feeling ruthlessly. She was so young and innocent, and yet she was shrewd and refreshing, with a good mind and a strong spirit. But she was not for him to take lightly and his mind acknowledged it. He had seen too much and lived too hard for their paths to meet again. She would love deeply, he felt, when she came to full womanhood and he must not—would not be the one to shatter her life with a careless affair. For that was all it could be.

And so he raised her hand to his lips with a slight self-mocking smile. 'One day, my lady, your own armoury of weapons will be a formidable power to strike down all the knights within reach—who knows—right up to the throne itself.'

Alyce smiled. 'You flatter me, Sir Gilbert, but your talk intrigues me. If the day comes when I must needs use a weapon of that sort to gain my end, then I will devise a new and novel method to fell my quarry in a way he least expects—but without emasculation, I promise!'

He threw back his head and laughed. The King looked over at them and smiled as Sir Gilbert kissed her hand again, saying with an appreciative gleam in his eye, 'I would not expect less, my lady, but either way I feel your quarry will not complain.'

He escorted her to a seat beside her father, then bowed both to her and the King. Alyce's eyes followed him, frowning a little, as he moved towards the marquees. He was so different from Roger, and yet she sensed that beneath his cynicism there lay a passionate heart that would one day engulf and scorch with a searing heat the woman who found it.

She saw him enter a marquee, then her eyes rose to the pennon above. The de Boveney device fluttered high against the blue of the heavens. And Roger was even now donning his chainmail, she supposed, visualising the eager face and glowing eyes as he waited his turn. Below the royal stand the heralds moved into position, the order of competitors finally arranged.

The trumpets gave tongue and the crowd quietened. All eyes turned to the King. He raised his hand. At that signal, two riders emerged from the marquees, one at each end of the field, accompanied by a squire raising aloft the personal standard of the combatant. Alyce leaned forward with clasped hands. Neither was the de Boveney standard. Roger must come later in the lists.

For over an hour the ground thundered under charging hooves, the crowd cheered and clapped, the crash of metal on metal and the crack of a breaking lance filled the air, but still the de Boveney standard was not raised. Rider after rider met and engaged, and the ground shook to falling bodies and the rattle of flying shields. Two horses went down but struggled to their feet unhurt.

Most unhorsed men were on their feet in seconds, bowing to the victors and to the King before trudging disconsolately back to the marquees. Others were helped off the field by their squires and grooms, suffering, it seemed from messages brought to the King, from only an assortment of sprains and bruises. Still there was no sign of Roger or the de Boveney standard.

'Father,' she asked, 'have we not seen Sir Lionel d'Eston yet?'

'Not yet, daughter. These contests are for those who prefer only to fight each other and not the champion. Those that have challenged Sir Lionel meet only him.' He glanced at the far marquee. 'It seems it is now time for the main bouts of the day for here is the master himself.'

LADY OF STARLIGHT 77

Alyce followed his gaze and bit back a gasp. A black-clad knight, waiting under a banner that showed an eagle with outstretched wings, sat motionless on a tall well-muscled destrier. The knight was enormous, his shoulders wide and strong under the glinting mail and burnished breastplate.

'By the Rood,' her father said admiringly. 'Now there is a man I'd not care to meet, though I were twenty years younger.'

Without a doubt this was the famed Sir Lionel. The contests began and Alyce's heart quailed within her as she realised the extent of his skill. Excitement grew intense as Sir Lionel unhorsed a succession of challengers with a deft thrust of his lance. He and the destrier moved as one, answering each other's movements as if welded together in one invincible force.

And yet his lance was controlled, plucking opponents from their saddles with a delicate kind of grace. No battering-ram, this knight, and Alyce could not help but admire his expertise. All his victims rose from the ground of their own volition, saluting him generously.

Alyce glanced towards the marquees, then her body grew rigid. A banner rose, unfurling in the breeze. Her heart jumped as she saw the de Boveney arms. Below, a white stallion, ears pricked, curvetted with eagerness.

She turned impulsively to Earl Robert, then caught back the words on her tongue. How stupid to plead for the bouts to be stopped! Her father would think her deranged. Once the challenge was issued, it could not be withdrawn without loss of honour, and Roger would never withdraw, she was certain.

Gazing at the lithe figure moving with the motion of the horse, she prayed that he might suffer little more than slight bruising. The trumpets sounded and the crowd hushed. Then de Boveney moved forward. It hardly seemed fair, Alyce thought wildly. Sir Lionel was twice the size of his opponent. Roger was mad to take on a man of such experience.

The riders spurred forward, clods of turf sprayed out from beneath the horses. The course had been churned to roughness and stones showed through the once-smooth turf.

Alyce's hands grew damp, and the noise roared in her ears. The earth shook to the pounding of hooves. Two lances dropped to the horizontal in unison. Twenty yards separated them—ten yards—five——

It was unbearable, but Alyce could not tear her eyes away. A tiny stone, hurled aloft by the destrier's hooves, flashed like an arrow within an inch of its face. The horse flinched and side-stepped momentarily, flinging up its head but still surging forward, its massive chest heaving. Aware of the loss of rhythm, Sir Lionel fought to turn the horse round upon itself and abort the meeting. He was out of position, his lance jerked too high. The riders were upon each other.

Sir Lionel, in desperation, sought to fling up his lance, but was too late. The tip of it struck the nasal guard of his opponent, twisting it sideways, but the force of the blow was barely deflected. The lance-point turned on impact. A white face was briefly glimpsed, then a gush of scarlet. The slim figure of his opponent rose on impact, then hurtled backwards, somersaulting over and over to crash and lie motionless on the grass.

He lay twisted and still—as still as death itself. A shuddering gasp ran through the spectators. Was this to be the first fatality of the day? Sir Lionel halted his plunging horse and threw himself from the saddle, running towards the crumpled figure. Stewards and competitors raced across the field.

In the sudden silence of tragedy, Alyce sat rigid, unbreathing, incapable of movement. Then a wave of horror swept up her body, blurring her vision. The scene before her wavered, tilted. The field spun madly. Her hands reached out blindly towards her father, and she fell into darkness.

CHAPTER SEVEN

ALYCE came to her senses lying in her own bedchamber. Edith was bending over her, holding a beaker.

'Take a sip of this, my little one,' she urged. ''Tis heartsease from your own infusion, and will put strength into you. I've mixed with it a little chervil to freshen the brain and cowslip to help you sleep.'

With a dry throat and a throbbing head, Alyce responded automatically and drained the beaker. Her mind was a struggling mass of impressions but the herbal drink confused her even more, and she gave up the struggle and drifted back to sleep.

When next she woke her head was clear. She lay still, staring at the rafters above, feeling a vague sense of loss. What had happened? She had been watching the tournament, she recalled. Memory returned, engulfing her in a tide of sick horror. Roger! Roger was dead!

She sat bolt upright, bringing Edith to her side quickly, alarmed by the wide sightless stare. Alyce brushed aside the offered beaker. 'Enough. What hour is it? I must go below. I must find out——' She stopped, appalled by what she might find.

'It is gone sundown, my lady, and the gates locked. There's no need to stir. My lord, your father, will be here any moment.'

Alyce stared about her, suddenly aware of the vast stillness. 'Why is everything so quiet? There are no voices from the hall nor sounds from the kitchen.'

Before Edith could reply the door opened. Earl Robert

stepped into the room, his eyes brightening as he saw his daughter fully conscious.

'Thank the saints you are recovered, Alyce. We thought you would never come to your senses.' He crossed the room and sat beside her bed. Edith curtsied and moved away.

'His Majesty left his best wishes for your speedy recovery, and bade me tell you he will not forget his promise.'

'Left, Father? I don't understand.'

'A messenger came, daughter, as you were being carried off the tournament field. Reports say that the Danes have gathered a great army and intend to wrest this realm from the King. With the help of his father-in-law, Robert of Flanders, King Cnut plans to invade us, so William has sent out his barons to raise the country. He has gone himself to Essex to inspect the coastal defences protecting the sea routes from Denmark.'

'They've all gone?' Alyce asked on a whisper.

'Every man of them,' her father said, smiling.

'But Roger—Roger de Boveney, Father, the knight slain by Sir Lionel. What of him?'

'Slain? What nonsense is this? Sir Lionel does not slay his opponents.'

'But I saw him fall, and he lay so still.'

'Merely knocked out of his senses by the fall.'

'But the blood, Father!' She choked and grew pale. He gripped her hands, fearing she would faint again.

'Nothing but a flesh wound, I assure you. Sir Lionel's lance took him across the cheekbone. It will heal in time, but he'll bear the scar of it for the rest of his days.'

'Truly, Father?'

'I swear on the holy relics that every knight, including Roger de Boveney, was in the saddle when they left.'

Alyce lay back, relief flooding through her. Scarred or not, she would always love him.

Her father patted her hand. ' 'Tis only natural for a young

maid to faint at such a sight, but you must put it out of your mind, my dear, and be strong, for if the Danes come we must hold this castle at whatever cost.'

As summer waned and the leaves began to fall, she heard of the vast army William had gathered to repel the threatened invasion. Soldiers were spread across the country, quartered with each of his vassals according to the produce of the estate, so that none knew great hardship. But hardship there was as lands were neglected while men stood to arms. Rumour and speculation were rife, but still the Danes delayed. Winter flung itself upon them and fierce winds swept in from the sea.

Each night Alyce lay beneath the bearskin and dreamed of Roger. When would she see him again? By day she was often to be found at the turret window, her eyes on the cleft between the now barren hills. One day the banners and hauberks, fluttering and glinting on the hillside, would flaunt their colourful passage and her knight come riding down to claim her hand. The King had promised.

But the King had other things on his mind, she knew, things of greater importance than the betrothal of a girl. The Danes were a strong and fearless race who had plagued the Saxon kings for centuries, raiding and pillaging the coasts. Even when they were paid tribute amounting to thousands of pounds, Danegeld they called it, it was never enough to rid the country of their presence. The coming of William of Normandy had united the country under one King, where previously there had been a number of Kings—even at one time seven Kings—each ruling a part and warring with each other. On occasions they had fought the Danes together but some had joined with the Danes to win their own personal battles.

Alyce was in no doubt that William could hold his kingdom, but her heart shrank from the thought of what it might involve. Heavy casualties could yet take Roger from her.

While the suspense went on, Earl Robert prepared his men and looked to the defences of his castle. Strangers were welcomed warily and there was little visiting between neighbours, each too busy preparing his own stronghold. She could have wished that Count Hubert was so engaged, but his visits continued as she had feared. Earl Robert was not displeased for he had a fondness for chess, that game brought from the East, and de Louches was an expert at the game.

Perhaps once a week there was an unwelcome visitor, and Alyce took care to retreat to her room immediately dinner was over. With Meg beside her she barred the door before retiring. Only then did either girl feel secure from the Count, although Alyce knew that with such a game as chess, played between two, no opportunity was afforded for the Count's presence anywhere but in the room they played.

But one evening, as Alyce asked leave to withdraw, her father raised frowning eyes to her.

'My dear,' he said on a note of reproof, 'our guest has begun to think his presence displeases you. What attractions are there in your bedchamber that you should seek it so soon after dinner?'

'I am sorry, Father, but I assumed you would wish to play chess as you always do, and my presence is therefore unnecessary.'

'My lord Count has expressed his distress that our games seem to drive you away.'

'He is mistaken, Father. I have no dislike of the game.' She stared at de Louches pointedly. He was smiling and she knew he understood her implied insult but he gave no sign. 'If you wish it, Father, I will stay and watch your game for a time.'

'Then let us miss play tonight, Robert,' suggested the Count, 'and enjoy the rare company of my Lady Alyce instead. It is not often I have the pleasure, and my castle is lonely for an unwed, childless fellow like me. These visits give me great joy, and there is little of that in my life. A smile from your daughter, my friend, is like dew to a parched flower.'

Earl Robert laughed. 'You sound almost like one of those minstrel fellows, Hubert. I would not have thought it in you.'

'Nor I,' said de Louches, his eyes on Alyce. 'But there is something in my lady that brings such words to my lips. I am not so old a bachelor that I cannot appreciate beauty and grace, but then you know how highly I esteem your daughter, Robert.'

'You have spoken of it, yes, but she is young. I would not wish to lose her yet.'

'You would hardly lose her, for there are barely two miles between our lands. Think what a holding that would be, to combine the two for your first grandson!'

Alyce had grown rigid, and her hands trembled in her lap. Her father had become thoughtful as he gazed into the fire. She might have known the Count would consider that prospect a greater inducement than all the compliments he might have showered on her. His rank was satisfactory, but could her father understand her dislike of the match? Might he feel that reluctance to become a wife was only to be expected of any young girl but once the thing was arranged, she would grow used to the idea? What could she say? She must speak.

'I am flattered, Count Hubert,' she said on an even tone. 'Perhaps I remind you of my mother, for they say I am very like her. I don't remember her too well, but I am sure you would recall her beauty for you were more of an age, I imagine. It was so many years ago.'

Both men were gazing at her as she spoke and she smiled innocently. Earl Robert's expression had softened slightly at the mention of his wife, but Count Hubert's eyes glittered angrily.

'Not quite, my lady,' he countered through clenched teeth. 'I was a mere stripling when your lady mother arrived from

Normandy. I admired her in my youth, as any youngster would, but now in full prime I can look back and recall, as you so rightly said, her beauty. With respect, my lady, 'twould be hard for any to come close. But you are fair enough.'

If he sought to discomfit her he was mistaken. Alyce smiled inwardly as Earl Robert began to talk of days in Normandy and the dangerous moment passed.

She encouraged him with eager questions until it was time for the Count to take his leave. But he would be back, she knew, to nurture the seed set in her father's mind. If only the King had not left so hurriedly! He could not have spoken to her father or she would have known it tonight. If Count Hubert showed signs of winning over the Earl, then she must speak of it herself.

In the week that followed, the rain fell without pause. The river swelled and burst its banks. Fording it was too perilous and the small stone bridge, the only other way to cross, was weakened too much to allow passage of more than one man on foot. Apart from the fact that several acres of land were under water and the peasants suffered the drowning of their late crops, Alyce could not help but be relieved, for it kept de Louches away.

But even that disaster was not long-lived, and her relief was short. The rains ceased and November turned dry. The river level fell rapidly, and winds from inland blew the dampness away. The sun reappeared, bringing with it a surprising mildness. When Alyce glimpsed in the distance masons at work on the bridge, she knew that before long she must face the Count again.

News of King William filtered through to them slowly. The Danes were still poised for invasion and the King's forces must hold ready. She almost wished the Danes would make a move, for this waiting time seemed endless. But then she thought of Roger and the last time she had seen him.

Apart from the scarred cheek he would look the same, perhaps leaner and a little older, for the life of a soldier was hard. No man could stay the same after witnessing the horrors of the battlefield.

Within days of the river bridge being rebuilt, Count Hubert was back to his visiting. Alyce thought of pleading a headache on that first evening, but decided against it. If de Louches reverted to his topic of combining the estates, she must be there to ensure that nothing was arranged without her knowledge.

She dressed with great care that night, choosing a high-necked tunic of thick grey wool that hid her figure. Her girdle she tied loosely to disguise her waist. The plain grey veil added nothing to her looks; in fact, it made her appear even younger than she was, almost nun-like, she decided with satisfaction. De Louches should have nothing on which to fix his lewd stare.

Her father's eyebrows rose a little as she entered the hall. He must wonder why she dressed so plainly, she thought. De Louches, lounging against the overmantel, was in contrast richly dressed, with a collar of heavy gold chain about his throat and several rings on his thick fingers.

After one glance and a slight curtsy in his direction, she seated herself by the fire, a strange feeling of unease overtaking her. Why was he so dressed, she wondered? It was not an occasion for finery. All through dinner she pondered, giving only brief answers to any remark addressed to her.

She discovered the reason when they retired to the solar. Her father remained on his feet, frowning a little, then he said quite suddenly, 'Alyce, my dear child, you have been honoured by an offer of marriage from Count Hubert.'

Her gaze flashed up. 'Have I, Father?' she asked flatly.

Earl Robert's brows drew together in perplexity, but he

continued, 'I think it in your best interests to consider a betrothal between our two houses. I wish you safely settled in these dangerous times, and near enough to your old home to be able to exchange visits. I shall not lose you then to some noble from a faraway estate, and what I have will naturally be inherited by your sons.'

So, the seed planted by de Louches had taken root after all. It was only to be expected that her father would prefer a neighbouring suitor, and although there must be twenty years' difference between their ages, a little thing like that was outweighed by the material advantages. But sons sired by Count Hubert? Never! If a servant girl could escape his clutches, then she with her rank and education should be equally resourceful.

'But you said on Count Hubert's last visit, Father, that I was too young to wed. I feel it too, for I have seen little of life. I have never yet been to court! I would be grateful for that chance of seeing more of the world before I am betrothed. A few months in the company of noble ladies would add much to my education.'

'King William holds no court at present. It may well be a long time before he does.'

'I am content to wait, Father.'

Count Hubert stirred restlessly. In a moment he would raise objection, knowing he dare not risk a delay in his desire to marry and possess her quickly as he had threatened.

Without giving him time to speak, she went on swiftly, 'I am convinced my lord Count would prefer a wife who had learned the refinement of court life to a girl barely out of the schoolroom. A well-trained hostess for his grand state is surely a prerequisite for matrimony?'

'That is not necessary in our case, my lady. Whatever you may require to know, I will take great joy in the teaching of it. It will be my greatest delight to instruct you in all things.' He smiled fondly and with meaning.

'I am sure it will, my lord, but the refinements I speak of can only be learned by example from another lady. In fact the court was a subject much mentioned during the King's visit.' She paused as if in thoughtful regret. ' 'Tis a pity the Danes must choose this time, for the King showed interest in me and my future.'

Let them make what they wished of that, she thought. King William had not actually invited her to court, but if they believed he had, it would give them pause, rather than risk his displeasure.

'So that was the meaning of his message to you, Alyce,' said Earl Robert.

'What message was that?' asked de Louches.

'The King bade me tell Alyce he holds to the promise he made her. He was away before I could ask more. Was your presence at court the subject of that promise, Alyce?'

Alyce lowered her eyes, thinking furiously. How could she phrase it without lying? As Roger's wife she would naturally go to court, and William had promised a husband, so there would be a basis of truth in her reply. 'In part, Father, but we spoke of other things too which I cannot reveal, for he spoke them only to me.'

She risked a glance at de Louches and saw a vein swell in his forehead, but he spoke calmly. 'You should not withhold such talk from your father, my lady, but speak frankly. To be secretive is not seemly in a maid, and shows a neglect of filial duty.'

Alyce raised her chin and looked coldly at him. 'It is not for you to judge me, my lord. I am not your wife nor even your betrothed. If my words displease my father, then you will allow him to speak for himself.'

'Exactly so, daughter.' Earl Robert shot an angry look at de Louches. 'You take too much upon yourself, sir. I have not yet given my consent to this marriage.'

'You delay because of some vague remark of the King?' de

Louches asked heatedly, trying to restrain his rising anger. 'I think my lady imagines it to signify more than a commonplace courtesy and is seeking to raise her importance.'

'You think we should ignore the King, de Louches?' Her father's voice was edged with unusual sharpness. 'He is not a man who forgets a promise, however small. If he troubled to leave a message for my daughter in the heat of departure, then I for one, will not dismiss it lightly.'

'A promise of what? A place at court where she may be fawned upon as the King's protégée? A court that is full of prancing knights who care for nothing save fighting and whoring? Would you trust them to respect her youth and innocence?'

'I would trust my daughter, de Louches,' Earl Robert said in a hard voice. 'Is that not enough?'

'Then you will not make her reveal the discourse she had with the King, so that we may verify the truth of her assumptions?'

'No! If my daughter has said the talk was confidential, then it will remain so. That is a true statement, is it not, Alyce?'

'Yes, Father. The King's remarks were for my ears only. It would not be right to break that confidence without good reason.'

'Then there is no further need for discussion. I will bear your offer in mind, Count, but until the country is at peace again and the King returned to make this matter clear, there is no point in going further into the subject of betrothal.'

Count Hubert de Louches left the castle a furious and frustrated man. He did not for a moment credit Alyce's story, but believed it concocted out of dislike for himself. She had balked him over the girl, Meg, but she would not balk him for a second time. When he finally had her at his mercy, he would derive an exquisite delight in changing that dislike into fear and terror.

He was not a man it was safe to scorn. One day she would crawl and plead with him, but to no avail. He had sworn to possess her, and revenge would be the sweeter for opposition. A place at court, indeed! Before that came about there would be a place of his choosing for the insolent wench!

After the Count's departure, Alyce crossed to her father and knelt at his feet. He had flung himself into a chair and was frowning fiercely into the smouldering logs in the great fireplace.

'Father,' she said, 'I cannot like the Count. I am sorry if it displeases you, but I know him for a cruel man who ill-treats his people. He is of a—a lecherous nature—and his female servants are made to suffer his abuse of them.'

'There is always such talk, child, from ignorant people, and you should know better than to listen to servants' gossip. Because of your treatment of him, the Count has gone away an angry man. I regret my own loss of temper too. He is an old comrade, and our estates border too close to risk a return to the feuding between nobles that plagued us in the past. I have been an indulgent father—over-indulgent, I believe—and this is my reward! Instead of asking you to consider the union, I should have gone ahead and arranged the match in the usual manner.'

He stared at her coldly. 'There had better be good reason for your stand. I would not press you for explanation in front of de Louches, but you must tell me in truth of the King's promise. I have a right to know.'

'Yes, Father. If the King had not left so hurriedly, he would have spoken to you himself, as he promised me after the bear hunt.'

'The bear hunt? What has that to do with anything?'

'It is the whole point, Father. You were in the courtyard when the King sent for me. The moment he drew my attention to the bearskin, I guessed what had happened because of the wager the de Boveneys had made. I knew which knight was the more determined to please me. I could not let him be punished.'

'I admit to being puzzled by His Majesty's manner, for I knew he was not angry.'

'But I did not! I believed the King to be truly angry. He had spoken during the banquet of finding me a worthy husband from his court, one of his bravest knights, he said. I believe he thought to test the strength of my interest that morning. Thank heaven my guess had been right!'

'I remember you answered bravely and was proud of your courage, but then he spoke too low for any to hear save you. What were those words?'

'He was pleased, he said, by my defence of the knight who killed the bear, and he promised to speak to you on the subject.'

Earl Robert's frown left him and he gazed thoughtfully at her. 'Quite a catch, my dear. I can see now why you were not interested in a union with de Louches. The de Boveneys are high in favour with the King, and I could not ask for a better match.'

'And you are not angry with me any more?'

'No, my dear, but if you had told me of this before, I could have informed de Louches and averted the unpleasantness of this evening.'

'I am sorry, Father, it seemed too——' She floundered for words.

'I know,' he laughed. ' 'Twas the same when I courted your mother. I spoke to none of my feelings, for they were too tender and precious to flaunt in the open. Is that how it is, my Alyce?'

She smiled at him gratefully. 'Yes, Father, exactly so. I wanted to hold the feeling to myself and keep it unspoiled.'

'Then we will not speak of it again until the King is free to redeem his promise. You are quite sure of your own mind and that of the knight?'

'Oh, yes, for I met Sir Gilbert in the stables afterwards. He confirmed my guess and told me of the victory when I dressed Sir Roger's wound. I knew then, beyond doubt, that I had chosen the bravest knight, and was pleased to have proved my love to the King.'

She went to bed, content that her father would no longer consider the match with Count Hubert of any importance against an alliance with the de Boveneys.

CHAPTER EIGHT

Out of courtesy, Earl Robert told Alyce the following day, he had sent a message to the Count's castle, informing him that he should look elsewhere for a bride; Alyce's future was already decided by the King.

'I told him only the bare facts, my dear,' said her father. 'I mentioned no names, so you have no need to be alarmed that I broke your confidence. It will remain between the two of us until the present danger is past.'

'Thank you, Father. Do you know how things are progressing with the King?'

'I expect to hear daily, for there has been no news for a week now. I feel we should have heard had there been a great invasion, but the Danes may be seeking some unguarded shore before launching their offensive. We have done all we can to prevent such a landing.'

The castle was well guarded, with men on the parapets day and night. No one was allowed to leave and no one entered without being challenged and identified. The days passed slowly but Alyce was happy enough in the knowledge that the Count was no longer a visitor. She waited for news as eagerly as Earl Robert.

Towards sunset one evening, the watchtower reported a rider heading for the castle at great speed. Alyce waited beside her father in the hall while the horseman was challenged, then allowed to enter.

'From His Majesty,' announced the steward. 'He has news for my lord Earl.'

The man was admitted to the hall. There were lines of

strain on his face and his dust-laden clothes proclaimed the distance he had travelled. Earl Robert's gaze moved over the swaying figure, the unshaven face and bloodshot eyes, and he motioned to a stool. The man sank down gratefully.

'Thank you, my lord. My horse was near to foundering, but I had to force the beast on to reach you in time.'

'What is your message, man? How goes it with the King?'

'Not well, my lord.'

'You mean the Danes have landed?'

'No, my lord, not when I left. But there are reports of raiding parties landing along the coast. His Majesty dare not split his army to deal with them in case the object is diversion only.'

'And what does he require of me?'

'That you take your men-at-arms to Pevensey and prevent a landing. Their longboats have been sighted heading in that direction. The tides will sweep them into the bay by midnight.' He staggered to his feet. 'Give me leave to be on my way, my lord. I take a similar message to the Count de Louches.'

Earl Robert nodded. 'Very well. You will be provided with a fresh horse. Go your way quickly and warn the Count.'

After the man had gone, Earl Robert summoned his captains to prepare the men for departure. The bailey was lit by torches as horses were brought out hurriedly and saddled. The armourers ran about with swords and pikes, soldiers struggled into chainmail, and after what seemed like chaos, the troops were formed up behind their officers. Earl Robert appeared on the steps from the hall and surveyed his men for a moment, then accepted his helmet and kite-shaped shield from his squire.

He turned to Alyce. 'God keep you, my dear. The castle is

sparsely guarded, barely half-a-dozen able men left, but you should be safe enough until I return.' He embraced her warmly. ' 'Tis strange, but Pevensey is where we landed that day from Normandy.'

'God go with you, Father, and protect you as He did on that day. We shall be well enough here if they raid only the coast.'

The drawbridge was lowered with a harsh rattle of chain. Earl Robert rode out at the head of his troops, the Beaumont standard raised behind him. As the last man crossed the moat, the drawbridge began to rise.

Alyce retraced her steps into the hall where the servants were assembled. There was much to do. Pallets to be brought down, linen to be torn into strips for use as bandages and all the herbal medicines to be gathered together. If a battle ensued, there could be many casualties brought back to be healed. She sent every man and woman scurrying in different directions, each allotted a special duty. Food and ale must be prepared for the returning men as well as medicines. The pitifully few men left to guard the castle were ordered to patrol as best they could, while keeping a sharp lookout.

By midnight all was quiet. No job was left undone. Alyce sat by the fire, attended by Edith and Meg. She wore a plain woollen tunic and her strongest boots, her hair plaited and tied behind. Nearby, on a table, lay a dagger. Against a Danish battleaxe it would be an ineffectual weapon, but the sight of it gave her comfort, although she was quite convinced that the local lords would put the raiders to flight and be back in their castles by dawn.

Edith gave a stifled yawn, and Alyce looked up, smiling. 'Go to bed, Edith. There is no point in you staying up all night.'

'I dare not, my lady. What if something should happen?'

'If it is to happen then it will, whether you are asleep or awake.'

'But I could not take off my clothes for fear of being caught unready.'

'Then go and lie on one of those pallets, fully dressed. I will call if I need you.'

'Very well, my lady, but I will stay near the door and fully awake, mind you.' She crossed the hall and lowered herself awkwardly on to a pallet. In a few moments she was fast asleep.

Alyce exchanged a smile with Meg. 'Poor Edith is getting old and stiff. She needs her rest. You should lie down too.'

'I will stay by your side if you will permit me, my lady. I could not rest easy until my lord Earl is home.'

'Nor I, so in the meantime we can——' She broke off, turning her heard towards the door. 'Did you hear something, Meg?'

'A shout, I think—but cut short. Perhaps the wind—or the man turned.'

Ranulf rose from a stool by the fireplace. 'I will go and see, my lady.'

In the quietness of the night, the sudden screech and rattle of the drawbridge chains startled them.

Ranulf paused. 'My lord returns?' he asked, puzzled. 'I heard no horses.'

'Neither did I. Perhaps the wind is strong and took away the sounds. But leave the door barred, Ranulf. We must make certain.' She ran to a slitted window, pulling back the hanging. The drawbridge was down—the watchmen must have recognised a friend—and there was movement in the courtyard. Torchlight criss-crossed the bailey as men ran here and there.

A long wailing scream turned Alyce's blood cold. She looked up in time to see the guard from the watchtower hurtle down to crash on the ground. The clash of steel reverberated, and the brief glimpse of a whirling war-axe drove the blood from her face.

'God save us, it's the Danes!' cried Ranulf in a high frightened voice beside her.

Meg's gasp coincided with a thundering crash on the barred door, repeated again and again. The tip of an axe-blade showed through. Alyce leapt for her dagger. 'Arm yourselves!' she shouted.

Meg sped to the wall and pulled down a short sword. Ranulf drew his own dagger and they stood together. No use to hide or run. They could be found wherever they were. In spite of their terror, they stood firm. Beaumonts do not die screaming for mercy, Alyce thought proudly. We fight until we are cut down.

The door splintered and the bar broke. The cold night air rushed in. On the threshold stood four men in rough tunics. Alyce's eyes rested on the horned helmets and she stiffened, bringing up the dagger. The first man to move tripped on the edge of a pallet and fell upon Edith, who woke with a startled scream.

She stared in a confused way at the face above her. 'My lady, it's——' she began, but the short sword rose, flashing in the torchlight, and stabbed down into the old woman. Blood gushed across her tunic and Alyce's despairing scream of protest died with the strangled gasp of Edith's last breath. The old woman lay still, her eyes wide and sightless.

Stunned, disbelieving, Alyce stood rigid in horror, then a wave of anger, hot and scorching, tore through her body. In a white heat of fury, she came to life. 'Murdering swine! Scum of the farmyard!' Her voice rang across the hall. 'What harm could she have done you?'

The man wiped his sword callously across Edith's lifeless body. His eyes fixed themselves on Alyce. He rose, and with the other three, moved warily towards them. They came silently, without words, and the cautious approach, like the circling of hunting dogs, almost unnerved the little group. All sound had died away from outside. Only the hoarse breathing of the men was heard. They moved apart, each approaching from a different direction.

From a few feet away, one made a feint towards Ranulf. The page struck out with his dagger but it was flicked from his hand by the edge of a sword. He gasped and lunged forward wildly. A fist came up and he was knocked sprawling.

On Alyce's other side, Meg was trying to wield the weapon she carried. She stabbed at one but he avoided her thrust and brought up his own sword, sending hers spinning across the floor. A blanket snatched from a pallet was flung over her and she went down screaming.

Alyce stood alone. 'Devil's spawn! Dung of pigs!' she muttered, almost without realising she spoke at all. Her eyes glittered amber-yellow, like a wildcat at bay. Her fear was gone. Only hatred was left—hatred of men who could plunge a sword into the helpless body of her beloved Edith and use violence on a twelve-year-old page. Meg was still screaming and fighting beneath the blanket, but pinned down hopelessly by the heavy body of her captor.

The three men were close now; still silent but watching every move of the dagger Alyce turned from side to side, while holding it firmly against her body. Let them get near, she remembered her father teaching her. Keep your weapon close to allow less risk of disarmament. Then strike from below.

All the time, she was backing away. The wall touched her shoulders.

'Base-born swine,' she jeered. 'What do you wait for? Reinforcements?' She knew they could not understand her words, but by the Rood, she'd take at least one with her when they struck!

It suddenly occurred to her that assassination was possibly not their motive. They took the youngest women with them, didn't they? To treat as slaves or objects of play for their men. Rather death here and now than that! She had not refused the Count only to fall into the hands of men with a similar motive in mind.

Somehow they seemed reluctant to move in. One had bent to snatch up a blanket, then stood waiting as if seeking an opportunity to render her as useless as Meg. The other two exchanged quick glances, and the centre man nodded.

He lunged forward and Alyce raised her dagger. Instead of answering his movement, she crouched suddenly and threw herself sideways at the man who had killed Edith. It was not the move they expected, and in that brief moment of surprise, Alyce struck hard from below. The sharp point of her dagger tore through the man's tunic and ripped into his body, to bury itself up to the hilt in his chest.

She had the fierce satisfaction of seeing his eyes glaze over as he staggered. The dagger was torn from her fingers by the strength of her thrust as the man fell backwards, then the blanket came down. She fought like a netted animal until a crashing blow on the side of her head sent her spinning into darkness.

It was the muttering that woke her. She regretted that, for her throat was dry and the noises inside her throbbing head were like the pealing of out-of-tune bells. Oblivion was better than this churning sickness and pounding in her temples. And beyond the steady thump was another sound. A hissing rhythmic beat that swayed her body, adding to the discomfort of the hard floor. The blanket still enveloped her and when she tried to push it away, she discovered that her hands were bound to her sides.

Her ankles too were bound. Trying to ease her position, she turned on to her side and came into contact with something that emitted a faint groan. It must be Meg or Ranulf—if they had not killed the boy after her capture. But where were they? Still lying on the floor where they had fallen?

Floor? Her mind began to clear and the sounds separated and became identifiable. This was no floor but the wooden hull of a boat, and the hissing noise was oars plunging smoothly in and out of the water. No wonder her body swayed along with her stomach!

The bells in her head grew fainter, and she wished they would remove this stifling blanket. Thank heaven, at least it was one of her own and clean. Any other might have reeked with an overpowering stench of the stables. How long had it been? She could have remained unconscious for minutes or hours, there was no way of telling. Were they on board a longship heading for Denmark? Or still in coastal waters?

Someone, soon, must remove the blanket. There was no escape in the middle of the ocean. But she hesitated to call out—the answer might be another blow on the head. The voices she heard were muffled by the blanket and she caught no sense in the words.

For a long time she hovered between sleeping and waking but the swaying motion never ceased. Was it day or night? She was thirsty and pangs of hunger were making themselves felt. Surely they fed their captives? She fell asleep.

When next she woke, nothing had changed except that her head was clear. Had her father returned to the castle to find the bailey strewn with bodies, the main door broken in and no sign of his only daughter?

What would he do? What could he do? Then Alyce thought of Roger and the tears started in her eyes. She would never see him again. Never delight to his kisses and never—never—become his wife!

CHAPTER NINE

Alyce came slowly to full consciousness. The darkness was still there. She moved her fingers experimentally and then her arms, but the cords were gone. She was no longer bound or enveloped by the blanket. Her groping fingers touched cold stone and she shivered, feeling the dampness of it. The darkness was absolute and very quiet.

Where was she? In some underground place, she guessed, from the dank, unsavoury atmosphere and the creeping chill. Alone? She forced her aching body into movement and achieved a sitting position. Even that little effort made her head spin, and she rested a while until her senses cleared. Then with arms outstretched, she turned, kneeling, and spread her hands. Straw rustled as she moved, releasing the stench of decades to rise overpoweringly to her nostrils.

Her searching hands came into contact with a body. She recoiled automatically, then forced her fingers to return. A shoulder—a face—thank God, a warm face—then her hands were caught in a spread of hair. Visualising the long fair hair, her heart leapt.

'Meg! Meg! Is that you?'

There was a movement, a slight stirring, a confused mumble of words.

'Meg, wake up. Are you hurt? Answer me, Meg, for the love of God!'

The words stopped. She felt the body jerk. 'My—my lady?'

'Yes, Meg. Are you all right?'

'Ah, my head! 'Tis like a devil's forge with Satan himself hammering on my skull.'

'Lie still for a moment to recover your wits. I must find out who else is here.'

She crawled past Meg on hands and knees, discovering a wall on which she rasped her knuckles painfully, then came at length to another body. Her hands moved searchingly over the still form. Small, short-haired, soft downy skin.

'Ranulf! I think I've found Ranulf.'

He took longer than Meg to rouse, but as he came to his senses he flung away her hand. 'Who is it?' he asked in a tremulous voice. 'Go away! Don't touch me!'

'It's Lady Alyce, Ranulf. Don't be frightened. You did well. Meg is with us, but who else I don't know. Perhaps no one.'

A male voice spoke from a dark corner. 'My lady, there are four of us here. We dared not speak before, for we knew not who you were.'

'Who are you? From the castle of the Beaumonts?'

'From my lady's kitchen, yes. I am a cook. There are two maids here and a boy scullion.'

'No one else?'

'I think they killed the others. All my lord's men-at-arms, anyway.'

'Do you know where we are? Have you any idea?'

'None, my lady, save in some dungeon below ground. I remember being carried like a sack of grain down a stair before being flung into this corner.'

A girl's voice spoke. 'I had come to my wits, my lady, to see something of this place before they took the torch away. It is empty of everything and was so when they threw us down.'

'You saw no window or other entrance?'

'I think,' the girl hesitated, 'I think, maybe a tiny barred window high in the wall, but too small and high to reach.'

'Well, even a tiny window will admit light, so I suppose it

is night-time outside. We can do nothing but wait until dawn. I expect even Danes will feed their prisoners unless they prefer dead ones, but why bother to capture us if that is their intention?'

She made her slow progress back to Meg. Ranulf had crawled to her side, comforted by the presence of someone he knew. There was nothing to do but try to sleep and wait for dawn. Unused to such a hard bed, Alyce was unable to relax for many hours, but at last she fell into a state of semi-sleep, waking frequently to ease her cold body.

Grey light crept slowly into the dungeon, revealing its seven inmates. Alyce opened her eyes thankfully. She had never liked utter darkness. Even in her own chamber there had been starlight or moonlight to relieve the blackness. But here, without either, and without the warmth of a soft bed and bearskin covering, there was only the comfort of dawn.

Her gaze travelled round the accommodation as she struggled to her feet, grimacing at the stiffness of her limbs. Beside her, Meg and Ranulf still slept. Apart from grime and general untidiness they appeared uninjured, although a bruise showed darkly on Meg's forehead. She felt her own head and winced as her fingers probed a sore place.

Moving across the floor, she gazed down at the four huddled in a corner. A middle-aged man, a boy and two young girls, as he had described. Why hadn't the man been killed, she wondered? Perhaps only those who offered resistance had been cut down. A soup-ladle was not much of a weapon against a battle-axe. Still, she was glad they had survived. Even Danes needed cooks and scullions. The maids, she supposed, were destined for the same fate as she and Meg.

The dungeon became clearer as the light increased. A small grilled opening set in the wall gave a view of sky only, too high to reach unless one was twenty-five feet tall. Even then, to what point? The bars were embedded in the stonework. One would need strong men and tools to remove them.

She heard the faint slap of water and realised that the window must look out over a moat but where she stood was below the water level. That accounted for the dampness. She shivered and wrapped her arms about herself, glad she had worn a woollen tunic. But they might have left the blankets, she thought, staring with distaste at the dirty, rush-strewn floor.

Ranulf woke with a start, dismay and disbelief on his face. She could see where tears had cleansed the grime on his cheeks and her heart went out to him. He was only a child.

'Oh, my lady,' he gulped. 'I thought it must be some terrible nightmare.'

'I only wish it was, but it is all too true, I am afraid.'

'What will they do to us?'

'I have no idea, but you may only find yourself serving another master,' she said, trying to smile. 'Don't worry. I am sure you will come to no harm.' At this moment she had no wish to dwell on the future rôle assigned to herself.

She sat with her back to a wall, facing the door. A small panel had been cut from the top half, but instead of a grille a solid wooden shutter was in place. Eventually, she supposed, someone would come. With food and drink perhaps, and orders to remove them from this place.

Meg woke, and then the others. Alyce recognised them vaguely, but she had had little contact with the kitchen people except through the head steward. She called them to her side.

'There is little point in keeping to our separate stations now,' she said. 'We are all the same here, all prisoners of the Danes. They will not care that I am an Earl's daughter or you the children of villagers. Our treatment will be just the same,' she smiled at them. 'I hope you will fare no worse than if you had been undisturbed.'

The man spoke. 'We were happy at the castle, my lady. The lord Earl was a good man to his people and we were proud to belong there. The Danes may not give you the respect of your rank, but we are not so base as to make that an excuse for treating you as one of us. You are still our Lady Alyce and we will serve you to our last breath.'

The others nodded vigorously, and Alyce was touched by their support. Her eyes were bright with tears as she replied. 'I thank you for your loyalty to my house. I am proud to share my captivity with you. If there is any hope of mercy from these people, I will do my utmost to plead on your behalf.'

They were disturbed by the sound of a bolt being drawn. All heads turned towards the door. Alyce was on her feet instantly. She approached the door. A face stared through the opened shutter, the face of a black-haired, bearded man. He met her gaze without expression.

'I hope you have brought food and water,' she said. 'Or are we to starve to death?'

There was no reply, only a blank look, then another bolt was withdrawn and the door opened. The man stepped inside, his drawn sword pointed at her as he stood to one side, allowing a smaller man to enter with a tray. This he placed on the floor and retreated. Alyce glanced at the tray. A large earthenware jug and one beaker stood on it, beside a dish containing bread.

The man with the sword moved backwards.

'Wait!' called Alyce.

The man stopped and looked at her inquiringly, his eyes narrowed in suspicion.

'It is very cold in here. Give us blankets before we die of it. We are not criminals and demand the rights of prisoners taken in battle. And what good is one beaker? There are seven of us here.'

Although she doubted he understood, he seemed impressed by her imperious tone. She was amazed when the smaller man returned after a few moments with an armful of blankets and another tray of beakers. As the door closed behind them, they heard the footsteps move away.

Meg let out a sigh of relief. 'You are brave, my lady. I liked not the look of that bearded one.'

Alyce laughed. 'Neither did I, but at least we know they want us to stay alive. Let us see what delights they have served us.'

Seven thick pieces of bread lay on the dish. The jug contained only water.

'The bread is fresh, my lady,' said the man as he bowed before her, offering her the first piece. 'But I would say the flour is of poor quality compared with that from our own kitchens. It has a different look about it.'

'Our bread was always good, but I confess to not thinking about it before. Being here with you has made me realise the work you must have done each day to provision our table. Tell me your names.'

'I am Wilfred, my lady, your head cook. These girls are Kate and Maud, and the boy is Edgar.'

Alyce smiled at them all. The girls were about her own age and the boy younger, perhaps the age of Ranulf. They sat silently then, each wrapped in a blanket—thankfully the ones from the castle—and ate their meagre breakfast. It did little to satisfy them, but was welcome.

'My lady,' Meg said thoughtfully, 'that Dane—he understood what you said.'

Alyce stared at her. 'You are right. I didn't think of it before. Perhaps he learned some English from captives brought here after other raids in the past. They were common enough at one time, before King William came. I believe Danes even lived in parts of England then.'

'I suppose they could have married English girls too.'

'Possibly,' agreed Alyce, and fell silent. The Danes were reputed to ravish rather than marry. What did the future hold for any of them? Surely they could not be left in this dungeon indefinitely? Someone, somewhere, must have had a reason for keeping them alive—some plan for their disposal. Although she dreaded what might come, could it be any worse than this?

As the day slowly wore on, the light faded and Alyce accepted that another night of darkness was in front of them. At least they had blankets now and were a little more comfortable, but hunger was still with them. They all acknowledged it, but as no one approached, there was nothing to be done.

By dawn they were all awake, restless with hunger and a little dirtier. The same two men arrived and the same breakfast was deposited on the floor.

Alyce lost her temper. Her head ached, she was hungry and dirty and quite unused to treatment of this kind.

'How dare you treat us this way?' she stormed at the guard. 'Do you think bread and water once a day is enough to keep us alive? We want more food and drink and water to wash in. And out of common decency, we demand you provide a privy and curtains too. We are not animals to keep penned in squalor.'

The guard stared at her silently, but his colour rose a little and Alyce knew he understood.

'You may tell your leader,' she threw at him angrily, 'that Beaumont pigs are housed in better comfort than this.'

She turned her back on him, shaking with fury. A sudden dizziness rose in her and she staggered to her blanket and lay down, feeling sick and weak. She heard the door shut and the bolt drive home.

It was some time before she felt better. Meg knelt beside her, coaxing her to drink and eat her slice of bread. Alyce complied wearily. It seemed that her outburst had brought no such results as it had before.

By the fourth day, she was too weak to even glance at the

LADY OF STARLIGHT 107

door when it opened. They were all weak and without the strength to do more than crawl from their blankets, but young Ranulf, huddled white-faced in his blanket and adding little to any previous conversation, raised his head and suddenly said in a high shrill voice, 'My lady is dying. She'll not see another dawn. You'd best bring a shroud tomorrow.'

The guard left and silence fell. 'Thank you, Ranulf,' Alyce whispered, her voice a hoarse echo. 'You did your best. Perhaps they intend us to die slowly.'

She turned her face into the blanket and tears of weakness crept down her cheeks. Her mind fell into a confused state, her thoughts wandering in a maze of half-dreams, half-reality.

A door opened, and a man's voice spoke. It must be her father. Was she ill? She felt ill. Was the tournament over? What had happened? She had felt herself falling. That was it. She was in her own bed and Edith was bending over her.

'Drink, my lady, it will put strength into you and then you can sleep.'

'I don't want to sleep. I want to go below. Take it away.'

But Edith was insistent. Alyce's mind jerked. There had been a dagger. She had seen the speed of it, striking down into Edith's defenceless body. How could she be here? She was dead, wasn't she? Then who was holding the beaker to her lips? No, that was part of the dream, for the light was bright in her eyes.

'You said it was sunset,' she protested, accusingly. 'The sun is shining. They haven't locked the gates.'

'My lady, drink this please, for me.' The voice had changed. It was Meg who spoke. 'Just a little, my lady. It's milk.'

Alyce's eyes fluttered open. 'Milk?' she asked dazedly.

'Yes, my lady. Let me hold you steady. There now, drink it up.'

It was all part of the dream, of course, but she drank obediently. It tasted like milk, so it must be. She stared up into Meg's drawn face and memory came flooding back. It was true then, and Edith was really dead. It was no dream.

'Meg.' Her voice was incredulous. 'Where did you get milk?'

'They brought it. A whole jug—enough for everyone. And meat too—there's twice as much bread in the dish. We've all eaten except you, and Ranulf is guarding your plate.'

Alyce's mind cleared. The milk had refreshed her and supplied a little strength. 'Guarding my plate?' she asked weakly. 'What nonsense! We don't guard things from our friends.' She managed to sit up and look into the worried faces about her. 'Ranulf,' she held out her hand, grasping his fingers warmly. 'Ranulf, thank you. It was your words that brought us food and milk. I will not forget that.'

Even as she spoke she realised how empty a promise it was. What could she do for anyone? She was as much a captive as they were and would receive the same treatment.

Meg was urging her to eat. It seemed pointless to cling to life, but they were all watching so anxiously that she knew she must make the effort. To renew her strength for what? But it seemed easier to do as they wanted than argue the point.

She ate slowly and without interest. The relief on their faces touched her and she smiled. The food made her feel better, and she had enough of the Beaumont pride to dislike the idea of dying like a rat in a cellar.

'Forgive my weakness,' she said. 'I know you have all suffered as much.'

'But we are more used to it, my lady,' replied Wilfred. 'We have known many times of hardship in the past when food was short everywhere. But our lord Earl your father, in his demesne, has always done his best for his people. We have been luckier than most. But you are gently born and unused to such hardship. It grieves me to see it.'

'What time is it, I wonder?' she asked. 'How long is it since they brought this food?'

'Perhaps an hour, my lady,' said Meg. 'And the guard who was with the servant came over and looked at you most closely. He seemed almost afraid that you might be dead.'

'It struck me,' added Wilfred, 'that he may have exceeded his orders and was fearful of what might befall him had you died under this treatment.'

'And what do you make of that, Wilfred?' asked Alyce, frowning.

'They know who you are, my lady, and the guard was charged with your life. When Ranulf told him you were dying, I caught a look of terror on his face. Whoever he serves, he goes in dread of that man. I feel that had you died, the guard would have paid with his life.'

'So I am of importance to someone,' Alyce said musingly. 'I wonder why.'

'Ransom, my lady,' said Ranulf suddenly. 'That must be it! I have heard of those things from the old times. The lord Earl will send payment and you will be released. It would do them no good if you were dead.'

'But why must I be kept in a dungeon if that is the case? Surely hostages merit some courtesy? If they know of my rank, why not house me in some comfort? I should be no less their prisoner.'

'Unless the man who holds you has some reason for this action,' commented Meg. 'Perhaps an enemy of my lord Earl, one who holds a grudge against him.'

'I can think of no one who hates him so much, Meg. Of course I know nothing of what happened before my father came to England, but that is twenty years ago. A long time to hold a grudge.'

'There are some who bear ill-will all their lives, and their sons continue the quarrel.'

'I think I should have known of such a feud, if it exists.'

From that moment the conditions of their captivity improved. Alyce's own weakness, brought starkly to their attention by Ranulf's words, seemed to have worked the miracle. Food was now brought twice a day. At times they discovered an extra pitcher filled with soup, poor enough stuff but containing a few vegetables. The diet was still sparse, but it gave them fresh heart and the feeling that starvation was not intended. In addition, a rough kind of privy was set up in a corner behind a wooden screen. But water to wash in was still denied them.

Two days passed, and with the improvement of their physical condition this inaction became irksome. From her blanket Alyce gazed at the high window, watching the winter sun stream through. Her strength was slowly returning, and with it a determination to put an end to their incarceration. The Danes must by now have had time to consider the future of them all, and, if Ranulf's guess was right, to have received some message from her father.

Heavy footsteps were heard coming along the stone corridor. More than one guard and the soft-footed servant, it seemed as they drew near. They heard the bolt pulled back and exchanged glances of surprise. It was not the hour for food. That usually arrived as the sun was setting.

'Perhaps,' said Alyce, 'the time has come for us to learn why we are here.'

The door swung open. Two men, strangers to them, stood on the threshold. Both wore chainmail and carried swords.

'Which is the Lady Alyce de Beaumont?' one asked in good English. He had no trace of accent, Alyce noted curiously. One might suppose him English born.

She rose and stared at him haughtily. 'I am Lady Alyce. Who are you, and what is it you want?'

'Come with us.'

'By whose orders?'

'By my master's.'

'And who is your master?'

'You will find that out when you meet him.' There was an edge of insolence to his voice and Alyce stared at him coldly, her eyes darkening with anger.

'Do your orders include using that insulting tone to me?' she asked icily. 'I am not in the habit of accepting rudeness from common soldiers. Unless your master is of your stamp, I will let him know of this lack of courtesy.'

To her intense surprise she saw him pale, and a hint of perspiration glistened on his face. His companion whispered urgently to him, his expression angry.

The spokesman swallowed audibly. 'I beg my lady's pardon. I did not intend rudeness. I pray you will overlook it.'

So he went in fear of his master, Alyce thought with satisfaction. How could she use that fear to her own advantage?

'That will depend,' she said clearly, 'on your own reply to my request. I desire my friends here to be supplied with water to wash in. A jug of fresh milk would not come amiss, either. And is it not time fresh straw was laid on this floor? We are none of us used to such disgusting conditions.'

'I—I will do my best, my lady.'

Alyce glanced over her shoulder at her companions. 'Be of good heart, my friends. I will see what manner of man it is who holds us.'

'God be with you, my lady,' answered Meg, and there was a murmur of assent from the others.

Alyce turned to the armed men. 'I am ready to meet this leader of yours. You may escort me to him.'

In spite of her filthy gown and unwashed body, there was an imperious lift to her chin. From under the matted hair her eyes glowed, large and luminous, from a face grown thin and haggard from imprisonment. There was a pride in her bearing that could not be disguised by any outward show. It was acknowledged without awareness by the guards as one stepped to hold open the door while the other bowed, without understanding why he did so. She was a disreputable-looking prisoner indeed, but for some strange reason there was a hint of awe in their regard as she swept past them.

The door was closed and bolted behind her. A long corridor stretched ahead towards a flight of stone steps. There were other doors in the corridor but no sounds came from behind them. Were they the only prisoners? she wondered. Perhaps the others had already met with their fates and only Alyce and her party were left to be disposed of.

A cold wind swept down the corridor and she shivered. It was better than the foetid atmosphere she had left, but in her weakened condition it had a bone-chilling bite to it. She thought briefly of her fur-lined cloaks back at the castle, then put them quickly out of her mind. By now they would be keeping some Danish woman warm in this November weather.

They traversed the corridor and came to the foot of the steps. One guard went ahead, the other followed as she began to climb. Even this small exercise taxed her strength. She paused, gasping, leaning against the wall. The guards exchanged worried looks. Alyce forced herself on. She reached the top, turned and beheld another flight stretching upwards. The wall she leaned upon was icy cold. Her body shook uncontrollably.

'Shall I carry you, my lady?' asked a guard.

Alyce shook her head wordlessly. She was determined to meet this leader face to face with her feet on the ground, not carried in and deposited before him like some worthless sack of grain. It took all her strength to reach the top of the steps and there she paused, her head swimming, her body one screaming ache of tortured bones.

They urged her on and she detected a fear in their manner. This leader must be a man of great stature to inspire such terror, she thought, but it was beyond her strength to hurry. He must wait, whoever he was. She could not have hurried for King William himself.

To her dismay she was faced by another flight of steps as they rounded the corner. 'God's bones!' she gasped. 'More steps? Does your leader live on the battlements, then?'

'That is where he said we must bring you, my lady. We only obey orders.'

'A week in his filthy dungeons, existing on kitchen scraps,' Alyce said bitterly, 'and he expects me to climb to the battlements. Does he think I am conditioned like a hunting dog? He should experience his own dungeons!'

'Please hurry, my lady! We shall meet with his displeasure. He said immediately.'

'Then hurry ahead yourself and tell him I follow,' she snapped. 'Why should I care if he tosses you from the battlements? I owe you no favours!'

The guard turned ashen. 'Do not speak so, I beg of you!'

Alyce stared into his rigid face. 'So that is one of his tricks, is it? I understand your fears now. Who, in the name of God, is this monster? Or should I say, in the name of the devil? He sounds blood-brother to that one.'

'I dare not tell you, my lady. He promised to flay us alive if we let fall any information. I have seen it done, and the sight is enough to turn the stomach.' The guard gazed up the steps with staring eyes. 'No more words, my lady, for he waits up there. Stay silent for your own sake, too.'

Alyce followed his gaze. She saw no one, but knew that whatever faced her, the answer was there.

Her heart hammered uncomfortably. Perspiration soaked her, even in the biting cold. It was one thing to be scornful to guards and servants who treated her ill, but whoever was up there had the power of life or death. He was not likely to be impressed by a haughty manner or sharp tongue. He could be a nobleman at the court of King Cnut himself, and impervious to her puny attempts at intimidation.

Softly, my lady, she told herself. Who had said that? It sounded familiar. Ah, yes, the day of the village market. Gilbert had grasped her bridle to restrain her impulsive move. She had hated him then for his curt ordering of her, but if only he were beside her now, she would obey without question whatever he ordered.

Roger, Gilbert, Gaston, Roland, she ran through their names longingly. But it was no use. There was no one to help her this time. She was alone in a far country. They were with the King, probably unaware even that she had been taken by raiders. The tears pricked her eyes but she fought them back, squaring her shoulders resolutely. This was something she must face alone and with all the bravery she was capable of mustering. If her fate was to live in dishonour, then she must do it with the pride of the Beaumonts to support her, while seeking the chance to end her life.

She reached the top of the steps, gasping with the effort, her vision misted by exertion. The late afternoon sun blinded her eyes but she saw the figure of a man. He had his back to her. He was leaning on the battlement wall, gazing over the countryside. Alyce clung to the rough stone, her eyes staring out over the wall. Trees, grass, hills, and below, a moat, water green and still, rubbish idly floating on its surface. For some reason she thought of ice and snow in relation to Denmark but it was only November. Perhaps the snow-capped mountains were inland. If this was a castle on the coast, the scenery could well be similar to their own.

'The lady is here, my lord,' said the guard in a subdued murmur. There was a wave of dismissal from the hand of the man, but he said no word.

Alyce waited, glad enough to rest and recover her breath. She could not see him clearly, but he was a tall man, heavily built and dressed in a long tunic that fell to his jewelled boots. A sword hung to one side of his leather belt, a dagger to the other. The arms leaning on the parapet were thick and well-muscled. The hair was short and dark. Another surprise, she thought, for she had imagined all Danes to be fair.

Alyce turned her gaze to the countryside. If he chose to ignore her, then she would do the same to him, and wait until he deigned to notice her presence. If it had not been quite so cold she could have enjoyed the view. A long expanse of heathland ran bare and uncultivated to a river. Beyond, far in the distance above a belt of trees, wisps of smoke arose as if a village or settlement lay behind.

She heard the scrape of a boot on stone and tensed, gathering together her strength. Turning slowly, she brought her gaze round to the man who was to decide her fate. He had turned too and now stood with his back to the parapet, his arms folded.

Her gaze reached his face and she started violently. The blood pounded through her head like blows from a hammer, then drained away, leaving her staring into the face of Count Hubert de Louches.

'Good day, my Lady Alyce,' he said, smiling.

With a mind spinning in disbelief and bewilderment, she stared speechlessly into the coarse, thick-lipped face. 'My—my lord Count—what do you do here?'

'Why, I come to take you as I promised, my little one. Are you not glad to see me?'

'Of course, my lord, but I never expected—I thought to meet some Danish chieftain——' She stared over the wall. 'How did you get here so quickly? Is my father with you?'

'No. Why should he be?'

'But the rescue party? Where are the soldiers? I heard no sounds of battle. How could this be accomplished without resistance?'

'There was no resistance, my lady.'

'You mean they surrendered without a fight? What kind of force did you bring?'

Count Hubert threw back his head and laughed. 'You look puzzled, my dear. I really believe you take this to be the land of the Danes.'

'But it must be! I remember the sea journey—the hours in the boat—the sound of oars throughout the night.'

'That can easily be achieved, my lady. You were rowed up and down the river to approximate the time taken to achieve the journey—and so you supposed you were in Denmark.'

Alyce pressed her hands to her temples. Was this some new, ugly dream? But the sight of de Louches was real enough. 'But the castle was attacked,' she insisted despairingly. 'I saw the Danes. They killed our men.'

'Yes, your castle was attacked, but not by Danes. A clever ruse, I thought, to use those old horned helmets I've had for many years.'

'You? You attacked the castle with your men dressed as Danes?'

'You've guessed correctly, my lady.'

'And the message taking my father to Pevensey? Your work too?'

'Of course. I would not wish to kill the Earl, just have him out of the way.'

'But you killed our men-at-arms and my old servant, Edith.'

'The killing of the servant woman was unfortunate. She recognised my man from the village, so she had to die.'

'And what did you hope to achieve by all this, my lord?'

'A silly question, my dear. I am sure you know the answer to that!' His smile was lazy but full of meaning.

Alyce gasped. No, it was impossible! She must be wrong, her mind wandering. 'You cannot have done all this in revenge for my father refusing your offer of marriage to me. That is too small a thing to warrant all this bloodshed.'

'I am a hard man when crossed, my dear, as you will learn.' He laughed harshly. 'As you have already learned in your dungeon, no doubt.'

Alyce swayed and gripped the parapet until her mind steadied. She had to believe him now. All this time she and her servants had languished in the de Louches dungeons, not in Danish ones. The misery and starvation had all been planned by the Count to break their spirits. She raised her head and stared over the wall.

'Yes, my dear,' said de Louches. 'You are a bare two miles from your castle, where your father sits alone.'

Her head jerked round. 'He will kill you for this,' she flashed hotly.

'He might if he knew, but he returned from his fruitless mission to find his castle broken open, his soldiers dead and his dear Alyce abducted by raiders. Instead of striking at Pevensey, the Danes landed at another spot.'

He spread his hands in mock desolation. 'I fought them off most bravely, I told him, but was powerless against such a force. I was unable to prevent them driving inland and reaching your castle, where they seized the Lady Alyce. To make it look authentic, we seized a handful of servants too. So now Earl Robert waits for a ransom demand that will never come.'

He paused, then continued slowly, his cruel smile mocking her despair. 'Already they are mourning you as lost, my dear. Accept your fate—for there will be no rescue.'

CHAPTER TEN

ALYCE stood for a long moment, staring into space. Two miles! Her father so near at hand, yet completely unaware of her plight. Count Hubert commiserating with the Earl, professing his own heartache while subjecting her to the indignity of his dungeons. Her gaze moved down to the waters of the moat. That was the way Meg had escaped, wasn't it?

'It would be pointless, my dear,' said the voice of the Count as if he read her thoughts. 'You would be taken before you had time either to drown or to escape. There is only one course open to you.'

'To accept my fate? A strange kind of courtship you perform, my lord.' She stared up into his face. 'Or does marriage no longer figure in your plans?'

'Oh, indeed it does, my lady, but not yet. Not until you have graced my bed for several weeks. Afterwards I shall call in the chaplain to perform the ceremony.'

From lacklustre eyes she regarded him, frowning. 'Why?'

'Your wits are very slow today, my dear. How else can I succeed to the Beaumont property unless you are my wife?'

'But I am mourned for lost, you said. My father will think me dead.'

'And I shall perform the impossible, discover your whereabouts in Denmark, secure your release by a surprise attack and bring you home victoriously. And out of love and gratitude, you shall beg the chaplain—who, of course, chose to accompany me on our search—to marry us during our homeward voyage.'

LADY OF STARLIGHT

'Do you think my father will believe that?'

'Why not? Captivity confuses the mind, lady, and there will be many witnesses to our journey. And you will still be my wife. He cannot dispute that evidence.'

'I suppose,' she said dryly, 'that all this could not have been accomplished without putting us through a week of hell and starvation in your dungeons?'

'You had blankets and were well fed. I could not serve you luxuries, or you would not have believed yourselves in Denmark.'

'Well fed?' Her eyes rose in amazement. 'You call that being well fed? I would hate to be a real prisoner if that is your idea of food.'

His gaze passed over her head and she saw his eyes narrow in suspicion as she followed his look towards the two guards waiting by the steps.

'Were my orders obeyed, Sergeant?' he asked in a menacing tone. The man nodded. 'Yes, my lord Count. We passed on your orders to the gaolers.'

'And you saw to it personally that they were carried out?'

The man looked ready to faint, Alyce thought curiously. He had not been near their prison. She could only assume that he had neglected to superintend the gaoler's treatment of them.

'I saw the food leave the kitchens twice a day as your lordship commanded,' he said. 'The gaoler took it down to the prisoners. There was plenty of it, my lord.'

The Count looked at Alyce. 'You said starvation. Was that just female exaggeration because your fare was not as rich as at your castle? Or have I been disobeyed? I make short work of disobedient servants, I assure you.'

Alyce glanced at the soldier. He had been the one who turned white when she mentioned being tossed from the battlements. The scorching words of protest died on her lips.

He had neglected his duty, certainly, and deserved punishment, but she could not condemn him to certain death.

The gaoler was the culprit, obviously. He and his assistant must have stolen the food allotted to the prisoners after it was handed over. She pondered for a moment, aware that the guard's eyes were on her in silent entreaty. It might be to her advantage to show mercy.

She turned back to the Count and shrugged. 'It is not the kind of hospitality I am used to, but I trust you will now make up for it by giving me the courtesy of my rank. There is no longer any reason for deception, I take it?'

'None at all. But first, my dear, you must earn that privilege. We will go now to my chambers, where I will teach you the first lesson.'

She recoiled from his clutch, staring into the coarse face and glittering eyes.

'My opinion of you has not changed, my lord. Do you imagine your bed is preferable to your dungeon? My answer is still no, so you may tell your men to return me there. I would rather die.'

'You had far better reconcile yourself to your fate, my dear. I have no intention of returning you to the dungeon. You no longer have any choice in the matter.'

'No?' she asked through clenched teeth, then her hand snaked out swiftly and grasped the dagger from his belt. She backed away quickly, the hilt gripped firmly in her fingers. 'I have this choice, my lord. Take one step nearer and I will kill myself.'

'Do that, my lady, and your companions in the dungeon will receive no more food. You complain of starvation? They shall know real starvation, until their flesh falls off and their bones rot.'

'They are innocent of any crime. Let them go! This matter is only between us.'

'And have them run to Earl Robert? You think I am wrong

in the head? Kill yourself, Alyce, and you condemn six innocent people to die slowly. Do you want that on your conscience?'

Alyce gave a harsh laugh. 'My conscience? What of your own, my lord?'

'I should suffer no pangs. They won't be the first to die down there, nor the last.'

'Have you no mercy in your soul? There are two young boys there, boys who have barely begun life, yet you condemn them to early graves.'

He shrugged. 'Peasants, every one of them, save your page. But they are mine to use as I will. Now stop this folly, Alyce, and throw down the dagger.'

'You think I will not use it?' Her eyes glared yellow from under the matted hair, and there was a strange intensity in them. He watched her closely without moving, a slight frown of unease on his face.

'You have the courage to take your life, I know, but it would be foolish sacrifice on your part.' Without taking his eyes off her he called, 'Sergeant! Bring up the six prisoners.'

The men turned and clattered down the steps.

'What do you intend now, my lord?'

'We will see how strong your resolve is, my lady.'

They waited in silence until the guards returned, herding the six before them. Alyce kept her gaze on the Count, afraid he would grab the dagger and overpower her if she glanced away, but he moved back towards the side wall of the battlements. She relaxed slightly and allowed her gaze to rest briefly on the prisoners. They were blinking in the sun, thin, haggard and as unkempt as she knew herself to be.

Meg's eyes widened as she saw Alyce with the dagger-blade pointed at her breast. She threw a swift, startled look at Count Hubert leaning against the wall.

'You may well look amazed, my friends,' Alyce said. 'But we are not, it seems, prisoners of the Danes. It was all a trick by Count Hubert.' She laughed a little wildly. 'We are all captives in his castle and at his mercy, but of that he has little!'

'My Lady Alyce is threatening to kill herself,' stated Count Hubert. 'I have brought you up here to dissuade her from this course. What do you say?'

'Oh, my lady,' breathed Meg, 'you must not.' She attempted to run to Alyce but was held back by the guards at de Louches' command. 'Why, my lady?'

'You, of all people, should know, Meg!'

Meg's pale face whitened even further. 'Holy Mother! He would do that to you—the daughter of Earl Robert?'

'We are all thought to have been taken by raiders, so none will come in search of us.' Alyce's eyes moved over Ranulf, Wilfred and the others. 'I am sorry to bring you all to this, but a few lives one way or another are of no account to my lord when he desires to achieve his objective.'

They stared at her in bewilderment, their eyes going from her to Count Hubert.

'But why is my lord Count holding us, my lady?' asked Ranulf. 'What does he want?'

'Me, Ranulf!' Alyce stated baldly. 'Count Hubert wants me in his bed. I can put it no gentler way. And to accomplish this act, he attacks our castle, kills our men-at-arms, takes us captive and puts it about that it was done by Danish raiders.'

There was a dismayed silence. 'What is to become of us?' asked one of the maids.

'That choice is my lady's,' responded Count Hubert, smiling at them. 'If the Lady Alyce carries out her threat, then you will all die, very slowly, back in the dungeon.'

'And if she lives, my lord, she is subject to your rape?' asked Wilfred.

De Louches glared at him, but Wilfred turned to Alyce. 'Whatever you decide, my lady, I for one will abide by your decision. I will not plead for my life at your expense. Let the others speak for themselves.'

'And should my lady accept your decree, what then, my lord?' Meg asked steadily. 'You cannot release us. We should still be your prisoners.'

'You would not go free, that is true, but life in my kitchens must surely be better than slow death in the dungeons.'

'Not much!' Meg retorted scornfully.

Count Hubert looked her over carefully. 'You have worked in my kitchens?'

Alyce caught Meg's eye and shook her head slightly in warning. With her fair hair lank and filthy, she was a far cry from the fresh-faced country girl with flowing corn-coloured tresses. Thank God, Alyce breathed, for the girl's quick wits as Meg hung her head and replied sullenly, 'No, but I have heard tell of them.'

'I, too,' said Ranulf, although his eyes were wide with fear. 'And I will stand by my lady.'

The two maids clung together and nodded wordlessly. Wilfred laid a hand on Edgar's shoulder. 'And you, lad?'

Edgar looked up into Wilfred's face and shivered. 'My brother came here as kitchen boy. We never saw him again. I will go with you.'

Count Hubert stared angrily at Alyce. 'Your servants are loyal, it seems, my lady. They would allow themselves to die of starvation in your cause.' He motioned to one of the guards. 'Bring my lady's page to me.'

Ranulf was thrust forward. 'Your name is Ranulf, I believe,' said the Count. 'You have great affection for your lady, do you not, boy?'

The page gulped. 'Y-yes, my lord.'

'I wonder if my lady returns your affection. Shall we put it to the test? Give me your dagger, Sergeant.'

Ranulf shrank back. 'What-what are you going to do, my lord?'

Count Hubert was smiling. 'Come closer, boy.' His hand shot out and he gripped Ranulf's ear. 'Will you have an earless page, my lady?'

Alyce stared, unbelieving. Ranulf squealed and fought to free himself. Count Hubert raised the dagger and slashed down. Not an ear but part of the lobe lay in his hand. Ranulf's scream rang through the air.

He clutched the side of his head and blood spurted from between his fingers. He sank to his knees, sobbing, his slight figure rocking backwards and forwards with pain.

De Louches glanced at Alyce. 'You are silent, my lady.'

'With—with horror at your bestial act,' she gasped. 'Leave the boy alone, I beg of you.'

Instead of replying he looked down at Ranulf. 'On your feet, boy. I will make your other ear a match and then I will take them both off completely. Pick him up, Sergeant.'

The Sergeant hesitated, his face pale.

'Sergeant!' thundered de Louches. 'Pick him up or you take his place!'

The soldier cast a helpless glance at Alyce as he bent to Ranulf.

'Wait!' Alyce called desperately, trying to gain time to recover her disordered wits. 'You said nothing of torture.'

'I have changed my mind in the face of their unconcern for starvation.' He grinned wolfishly. 'Perhaps you will change yours, my lady, when you see what I can do. Allow me to tell you. First, I shall carry out my promise to Ranulf, then do the same to the man and other boy. After a night of pain in the dungeon, I will hang all three in the bailey tomorrow. The girls I will give to my roughest soldiers—but only after I have done with them myself.'

There was a long painful silence, as if everyone held his breath. Alyce had no doubt that de Louches could carry through this threat if she continued to defy him. Even taking her own life was pointless now if it meant that six innocent people would die agonisingly. There was no longer any way she could help them, except by complying with his demands. But was she to throw down her dagger meekly and be dragged to his chamber, violated as she was, filthy and dishevelled?

An idea began to stir in her mind. She could but try it.

'And supposing I made no move to stop your cruelty, my lord,' she asked, 'but killed myself just the same? All your threats and punishments would come to nothing and your grand scheme be foiled. You would be no better off than if you had accepted your dismissal the last time we met.'

She caught a hint of blank disbelief in his eyes, then he frowned heavily and his lips twisted in mockery. 'But will you risk your resolve holding out, my lady?'

'Will you, my lord?' she asked softly.

He stared at her through narrowed eyes. She was still the proud lady, he thought. There was no sign of her crumbling under his threats. He had expected instant capitulation but had, it seemed, misjudged her resolve.

'And if I only return them to the dungeon unharmed, what then, my lady?'

'My answer is still the same.' She waited, wondering if her timing was right. 'Unless——' She let the word drift slowly away, praying that in his eagerness he would grasp it.

He was silent for so long that her spirits sank. Had she mistimed the moment?

'Unless—my lady?'

Her heart leapt exultantly, but her expression remained calm. She began to draw in the bait gently. Her eyebrows rose to their highest level, her voice became haughty. 'I am of noble birth, my lord, the daughter of an Earl. I ask you to remember my rank and not expect me to behave like some common tavern wench. You are a gentleman of noble birth yourself, and should not presume to treat me as such a wench. When I am bedded, my lord, it will not be in squalor, bearing the filth and smell of the dungeon. I am a lady, and will not be taken as I stand, without preparation.'

'Isn't that for me to decide, my lady?'

Had she gone too far? Alyce wondered. But then she saw his eyes, glittering with hope.

'Not if you observe my rank, my lord. In my present condition, I would be as lifeless as if I were dead, and what satisfaction would that bring you?'

'And what is it you want, my lady?'

'Nothing out of the ordinary, my lord, for a lady of birth. A few days' grace in private chambers where I may rest and regain my strength. A bed with clean sheets, hot water and perfumes and my servants about me. Is it too much to ask—considering the gains you envisage in the future?'

He regarded her thoughtfully. If he granted her request, it might hold him in good stead in the future when he revealed her to the Earl. To force her now, in all the filth and weakness of her body, would afford no satisfaction. It could turn her from him irrevocably, and she might still carry out her threat, given the chance. But to give her cause for gratitude would be a step in his favour. She was not a village wench but a lady, as she had stressed. He must curb his impatience. There was no escape for her. His reward could be the sweeter for allowing her the trappings of respectability.

'Very well, my lady. I will be generous because of your rank and my respect for your courage. I accept your conditions, and will give you two days' grace. You will come to me at sunset the day after tomorrow. My only condition to you is that you come willingly to my arms that night. Swear your solemn oath on it, lady, that my forbearance will not be in vain.'

'I swear to you, my lord, that on that night you will receive all that I can give.'

'Then you shall be housed in the turret room yonder. It leads nowhere but to these battlements, and your door will be guarded day and night. Food will be brought to you, and any request will be transmitted to me by the Sergeant here. No tricks, my lady, or you will strain my kindness and render your conditions void. Is that understood?'

'If you will swear an oath in return, my lord, that I and my household shall be unmolested by any during the time you have stated, then your kindness will receive its due reward.'

He stared into her face for a long moment but saw in the amber eyes no hint of guile or cunning. He should have remembered the cursed pride of the Beaumonts and handled it differently, realising that honour was more precious than life to them. But he would gain his objective all the same, and if a little luxury was all it took to save her pride, then he could afford to bestow it.

He waved his hand to the arched entrance of the turret.

'Your quarters, my lady. You will find them reasonably furnished, for it was turned into accommodation when I held a French hostage some time ago for the King. It is not large, but will serve for the two days before you move into my chambers. My Sergeant will escort you.'

Alyce inclined her head graciously, and not until Count Hubert's retreating footsteps had died away did she move.

'This way, my lady,' said the Sergeant. 'But first the dagger, if you please.'

She handed it over reluctantly, and he walked ahead as the small party came together and followed. A stout door had been fitted just inside the turret arch and a heavy bolt secured it. The Sergeant opened the door and stood aside.

Alyce entered her prison. Turrets did not ordinarily have windows, but a small one was set on the inner side wall overlooking the battlements: out of consideration, she supposed, for the unknown Frenchman. At least there would be light. The room was fairly large, a bed and chest stood by one wall, a small table and stools by another, while a screened area provided washing facilities. A wooden ladder stair rose to an upper level.

'There is a smaller room above, my lady,' said the Sergeant, 'where the men can sleep. I will have pallets and blankets sent up.'

Alyce examined the bed. 'You heard my request to the Count? Sheets and bed curtains for privacy, if you please, together with many jugs of hot water. We shall require fresh clothes, a small brazier for heating and fresh rushes on the floor. And, of course, a dressing for my page's injury.'

She smiled at him in a friendly fashion. She had seen his reluctance to deliver Ranulf to the Count's knife. Perhaps she might win him to her cause if she showed no hostility. He might hate Count Hubert just enough to overcome his fear and help them.

'I—I will do all in my power to make you comfortable, my lady,' he replied awkwardly, bowing himself out. She heard the bolt shoot into position, then she turned to face her companions.

'Well, my friends, we have gained two days' grace and for that we must be thankful.' She drew her page forward. 'My poor Ranulf! You have suffered worst of all. I am proud of you.'

'It is nothing, my lady,' he replied, trying bravely to smile. 'It hurts less now.'

CHAPTER ELEVEN

Servants soon arrived to carry out Alyce's orders. Her bed was made up with fresh linen, curtains hung from the four posts, the floor swept and strewn with clean rushes. Pallets and blankets appeared, together with steaming pitchers of water. The Sergeant himself prepared and lighted the brazier.

He moved over to Alyce. 'My lady—,' he began, haltingly, keeping his voice low, 'why did you hold your tongue about my treatment in the dungeons? I neglected my duty and deserved a flogging for leaving the serving of food to the gaoler and his lackey. You did not denounce me, yet I deserved your hatred.'

'Having you flogged would not alter my position, would it?' She looked at him curiously. 'You serve the Count, yet I feel you do not entirely share his nature.'

'I serve him because I must, for the sake of my family. He owns the land and the livelihoods of many—my family would be turned out to starve if I disobeyed him. We are not all like those who were sent to your castle, yet I feel great shame for what has happened. But I dare not help you, my lady.'

'But would you hinder me, I wonder?' she asked with a half-smile.

His eyes widened. 'There is no way you can escape, my lady. The Count will make very sure of that.'

'I know, but supposing I did—would you raise the alarm, or discover you had business in another direction? I speak in jest, of course. You understand that?'

He nodded. 'I have many duties about the castle, my lady. I cannot be expected to attend to them all at once. If something happens, it may take me quite a time to reach that place.'

Alyce smiled. 'Why, you could be on the other side of the castle completely, with no knowledge of what is going forward.'

'Exactly, my lady. You understand the situation perfectly.'

'Indeed I do. And you may—sometimes—have difficulty in finding Count Hubert and making your report.'

He regarded her without expression. 'It is a very big castle,' he murmured.

She thought of the Count's warning. No tricks, or the conditions are void. Was she being foolish in talking to this man? There was only one way to find out.

'Of course, if I should suddenly receive a visit from Count Hubert before the allotted time expires, I shall have no alternative but to acquaint him with certain facts.' She watched his eyes closely, but his regard did not waver.

'You would have every right, my lady, but he will not come save on his own account, and that he will hesitate to do lest he lose the advantage he holds.'

After he had gone, Wilfred, Ranulf and Edgar took their hot water and clothing up the ladder, leaving Alyce, Meg and the maids to strip off their filthy tunics. Behind the screen was a large, shallow pan, large enough for Alyce to sit in and enjoy her first wash in over a week.

In spite of their situation, she heard the two little maids giggling as they helped wash each other's hair in the buckets provided, exclaiming over the dirtiness of the water when they had finished. Alyce emerged in fresh woollen tunic and sandals, joining the others round the brazier as they dried their hair. Meg's corn-coloured tresses were revealed once more as she bent her head, drawing the bone comb through the shining strands.

'Oh, Meg!' exclaimed Alyce, remembering. 'I think, for your own safety, it would be as well to cover your hair with a kerchief while the Count's servants are about. The promise he made to me will not hold with you. If you should be recognised——' She gazed at Meg, her expression full of meaning.

The girl paled a little. 'You are right, my lady. When I caught your look on the battlements, I thought you were warning me not to anger the lord Count. I understand now. I will bind my hair so tightly that not one strand will show.'

'And stand away from the light whenever anyone enters,' Alyce added.

At that moment, Ranulf's voice floated down to them. 'May we come down now, my lady, if you are ready to receive us?'

'Yes, Ranulf, quite ready.'

They were joined by the men and Alyce looked with interest at the Beaumont servants. Wilfred was about forty, lean and grey-haired. Edgar, a fair-haired child, even younger than Ranulf, was small and bony with a freckled face and startlingly blue eyes. She glanced at the maids. What were they called? Ah, yes, Kate and Maud, both brown-haired and round-faced. Normally plump, she imagined, but the week of privation had stripped them of flesh. Ranulf's ear was heavily bandaged, but he seemed to be over the shock.

'Come to the fire, my friends, and dry the chill of the dungeons from your bones.' How strange, she thought, that I should call them friends. Yet they had become dear to her, and not just because she felt responsible for their plight. She was still their lady. Not even a week of complete equality below ground had changed their attitudes. The breath caught in her throat as she smilingly surveyed them, and her lips trembled.

'If I am forced to become mistress of—of this castle, I shall insist that you all remain members of my personal household. And if ever an opportunity to escape presents itself, I implore you to take it instantly. If you are gone one day, then know that I have wished you Godspeed. There is no other way I can repay your loyalty.'

'If one of us should escape, my lady,' said Wilfred, 'our first call will be to the lord Earl, your father.'

Alyce smiled sadly. 'Yes, I should like him to know I am alive, then he may cease grieving. But there will be little he can do once I am wedded to the Count.'

There was a knock on the door. Meg snatched up a kerchief from the heap of clothing on the bed and fled up the ladder.

'Come in,' called Alyce, as the girl disappeared upstairs.

The door, opened by the Sergeant, admitted a line of servants bearing trays of food. The smell of meat and fresh bread was unbelievably good to the occupants of the room. A cloth was thrown over the table, horn-handled knives laid out beside wooden platters, and pewter dishes filled with vegetables, roast pork and slices of beef filled the centre space. The scent of spiced wine rose as goblets and a jug appeared beside a basket of bread.

The Sergeant cast an eye over the table and seemed satisfied as the servants filed out. 'Your dinner is served, my lady,' he said, bowing. 'I hope this will be more to your liking than previous meals. You will not be disturbed again tonight.'

'Thank you, Sergeant. It looks splendid.'

As soon as the door had closed behind him, Meg peered over the ladder then descended, her eyes lighting up as she saw the food. Alyce had seated herself at the table before realising that only Ranulf had followed, to fill a goblet of wine which he then set by her plate.

'Will you take pork or beef first, my lady?'

LADY OF STARLIGHT   133

'I will take nothing if you expect me to eat alone.'

'But my lady, we cannot——'

'Nonsense! Forget our positions and come to the table, all of you. The food would grow cold and we are all hungry. I command you to join me. Will that do?'

No one argued. Stools were dragged up to the table and everyone ate, with only a little restraint in their bearing which was soon forgotten in the joy of eating well-cooked food. In a short time the dishes were empty, and Wilfred rose to light the wall sconce as the night drew in. Alyce yawned. Suddenly she felt desperately tired. Her body began to shake with reaction from all she had endured that day, since her first meeting with Count Hubert and discovering his trickery.

'I will help you to bed, my lady,' murmured Meg, noticing her condition. At her nod, Wilfred and the boys wished her goodnight and retired up the ladder. The two maids moved to the corner where their pallets lay. Meg removed Alyce's tunic and sandals, then tucked her into bed before dousing the light and seeking her own pallet. Only the glow of the brazier lit the room and that faded as Alyce sank into a dreamless sleep.

She woke refreshed from her night in the comfortable bed, the first night in a week when hunger had not disturbed her dreams. If only tomorrow might be delayed indefinitely, she could almost be happy. But the promise made must be kept. She owed it to her companions to put their safety before her own honour, for they had demonstrated their loyalty so strongly that she must protect them in the only way left open.

The Count, it seemed, intended to honour his side of the bargain. Hot water and food arrived promptly and the brazier was replenished. The company gathered once more round the table. They were more disposed to conversation than on the previous night, and even little Edgar ventured a remark or two, under the benevolent eye of Wilfred.

When the servants returned to remove the dishes, the Sergeant said in a low voice to Alyce, 'Hold back the ale and goblets, my lady. I will send a scullion to collect them presently.' His voice held some kind of message. Alyce was unable to fathom its meaning, but she obediently requested the servants to leave the jug and goblets.

Some two hours later there was a tap on the door. It opened slightly, a figure slipped in and the door closed. The bolt was heard to shoot into place.

Alyce raised her head, wondering why the Sergeant himself had not entered. She stared at the young man in rough, stained clothing, the unshaven face and unevenly cut hair. Why a scullion to remove the ale jug?

Behind her she heard a gasp, an incredulous murmur, then Meg flung herself across the floor and into the arms of the scullion. The man raised one warning finger to his lips, while his free arm encircled Meg's waist. Alyce knew then. She recognised the scullion as the young soldier who had watched Meg being prepared for a whipping in the market place. But a scullion?

'Harry!' Meg whispered. 'My lady told me of the dagger at your back that day. I never thought to see my husband again. Did he punish you? What happened? Why are you here?'

'All in good time, my love,' Harry said fondly. 'I am here by the grace of the Sergeant to try and help the Lady Alyce in return for her goodness to you. I am no longer a soldier—the Count considers me untrustworthy, so I am banished to the kitchens. I cannot leave the castle, I am watched too closely, but I am determined to think of some way to prevent my lady suffering the fate my lord Count intended for you.'

'Your thought is a kind one,' returned Alyce with a smile. 'But unless you have an army at your command, I can see no way out of our predicament.'

'Not an army, my lady, but I still have a few friends. Most here hate the Count, but are too afraid to move against him.'

'Then what can you do?'

'I don't know yet, but I am not watched after dark when the gates are closed. I will try to discover some other way out. I cannot come again today, it is too risky, but tomorrow at this time you will see me. I will tell you then if I have made any progress. I must go now, or the Sergeant may get into trouble.'

He gripped Meg's hands, kissed her swiftly and was gone as soon as his soft knock on the door had been answered.

Meg returned to the table amidst a hushed buzz of speculation from the younger ones, her face glowing with tenderness and hope. Alyce met Wilfred's eye and smiled. Neither had faith in a miraculous escape, but neither made any attempt to damp down the enthusiasm created by Harry's visit.

That night Alyce climbed into bed, still convinced that the next bed she reclined in would be my lord Count's. One scullion, even with moral support from the castle servants, was no match for the cunning de Louches.

She woke the next day even more convinced as time wore on and Harry did not make an appearance. By afternoon, even Meg was subdued. The shadows grew longer and Alyce knew that time was running out fast. They had all given up hope when a soft knock fell on the door, and a dark figure slipped in.

'I can only stay a minute, my lady,' Harry gasped. 'I have devised something, but I cannot do it until it grows dark and the gates are locked. You must go to the Count, my lady, and keep him at dinner for as long as you can. We have prepared many courses and there will be much wine. But I need time. You must try to give it to me.'

He was gone before any could speak. There was a long silence. It was broken by a knock on the door, and the Sergeant walked in carrying a wrapped bundle. His face was impassive as he laid it on the bed.

'My lord Count has sent you evening clothes, my lady. He asks that you wear them and join him in one hour's time. I will wait outside to escort you to his chambers.'

He paused, looking down at her. She read compassion in his gaze. 'May Our Lady's mercy go with you.' He left the room and the bolt grated.

One hour, thought Alyce. One hour to degradation and bitter defeat. She raised her head. If this was her fate, she would not go as a supplicant, begging mercy, whining like a beaten cur. She would meet de Louches proudly as her blood demanded, flying her standard bravely. He should not have the satisfaction of seeing her cowed and craven, whatever humiliation he planned. A Beaumont never asked quarter. She would not bring shame on that proud name.

Her resolve wavered as Meg revealed the gown he had sent. Wilfred, in kindness, ushered the boys and the young maids upstairs, leaving Alyce alone with Meg as the parcel was opened. Meg was aghast and Alyce's cheeks flamed with anger.

The tunic was of white silk, sleeveless, the neckline plunging almost to the waist, and was made from such delicate clinging silk that when held up to the light it was practically transparent. No undergarments were in the parcel, merely jewelled sandals, a chain of gold and a silk cloak.

'You cannot wear this—this costume, my lady,' said Meg. 'It's not decent.'

'I imagine that was the idea,' Alyce said, dryly. 'It puts me at an immediate disadvantage. I would rather wear this tunic I have on, but if I am to spin out the time as your Harry suggests, I can hardly help my cause by angering the Count at the outset. So I will wear it—but with a kerchief round my shoulders. I can always claim that the gown is too cold for November. Now, help me prepare, Meg.'

With her dark hair shining and loose about her shoulders, the long silk tunic moving softly round her ankles, she placed the chain over her head. The gold links lay coldly on her bare skin, reaching from neck to waist. Meg added the kerchief and reached for the cloak.

'God be with you, my lady,' she whispered as the sound of footsteps reached them. Both girls were white to the lips, rigid as marble statues as the door opened.

'It is time, my lady,' said the Sergeant softly.

Alyce nodded and followed him, unable to speak. On the battlements she paused, gazing over the countryside. The horizon was streaked with pink and gold, the sun almost gone. Her eyes rose to the first cluster of stars. Starlight on the battlements. She took a deep breath, trying not to think of that night she had planned to share with Roger, frustrated by the King's insistence on wrestling. Wherever Roger was, it was too late for them now.

She followed slowly as the Sergeant led her down a flight of steps and along a corridor. From an open doorway she felt the heat of a fire, and the scent of perfumed rushes rose to her nostrils. She smiled wryly. De Louches had thought of everything. How could she complain of the cold and keep the kerchief round her shoulders in the face of such heat? Her chin rose as she entered the room and gazed about her.

A table by the fire was laid for two, silver plate and goblets sparkling in the glow of candles. From a chair, the figure of Count Hubert rose.

'Good evening, my lady. That will be all, Sergeant. Let me take your cloak, my dear.'

He advanced upon her and she stood silently, flinching inwardly at the touch of his thick fingers on her neck as he removed the cloak. His eyes fell on the kerchief. She moved swiftly away, holding out her hands to the fire.

'Your battlements are cold, my lord. I will retain the kerchief until I am warm again.'

'As you wish,' he replied, his eyes moving over her with blatant interest. She suddenly realised that her figure must be outlined against the fire and moved quickly to a chair and sat down.

'I understand you have prepared a special dinner in my honour, my lord. Perhaps a glass of wine first?'

'Wine? I did not know you cared for wine.'

With a lazy smile, she gazed full into his eyes. 'There are many things you do not know about me, my lord, but you will learn in time.'

He returned her smile. 'And tonight will be a night for learning, eh, my lady?'

'Exactly. So let us make of it a special occasion and not rush the preliminaries, my lord. I hope your wines are French?' Her brows rose in enquiry.

He moved to a side table and filled two goblets, handing her one before taking the chair opposite. Alyce sipped her wine, conscious of the greedy eyes on her.

'How go things with the King, my lord?' she asked calmly. 'Does he still stand to arms?'

He threw her a puzzled glance. 'Well enough, I believe. The Danes still waver.'

'Perhaps they wait for Spring weather,' she replied and took another sip. She sensed his puzzlement. Had he thought to find her shrinking, tearful, full of pleas for mercy? The longer she kept him wondering, the better. She asked for more wine. It made her head spin a little, but perhaps it was a good thing. Her feelings would be dulled when he finally took her.

The meal lasted a long time. She noted his surprise as course after course appeared on the table. As the sweetmeats were brought in, she could see his reddened face growing more impatient by the second. She chose a sweetmeat and nibbled it delicately, then reached for another.

It must be full dark outside, she thought. Harry had pleaded for time. Surely he had had enough time to do whatever he planned? And yet there had been nothing to disturb the peace, and Count Hubert's patience was coming to an end. In another few minutes he would order the table cleared and the servants out. She drained her goblet recklessly, and held it out to be refilled.

Count Hubert lifted the flagon then rose and placed it deliberately on a side table. 'You have had enough to drink, my lady. And I hope enough to eat.' He clapped his hands and the servants entered. 'Clear the table and go back to the kitchens.' They obeyed. Through the open door, Alyce saw the Sergeant. Count Hubert raised his voice. 'Close the door, Sergeant, and see that I am not disturbed again tonight by anyone.'

'Yes, my lord.' The man avoided Alyce's gaze and the door closed.

'Now, my lady. From your flushed cheeks I would say you are warm enough to dispense with that kerchief.' His hands reached out and drew it from her neck. His gaze rested on the soft white skin of her breasts and his fingers traced the path of the chain. 'A very becoming gown, my dear. I knew it would suit you.'

'Did you have it specially made for me? Who made it? Do tell me, my lord.'

'Have done with questions, Alyce. Do you take me for a fool? I allowed you to linger over dinner to save your pride. Now it is over and high time you kept your side of the bargain.'

'All right, my lord, but another glass of wine first.' She felt deathly sick already, but still her mind was not dull enough to kill the inward flinching from his touch.

His hands grasped her shoulders. His eyes stared into hers. 'You'll be conscious when I take you, my lady,' he said savagely, 'not sprawled about like some drunken whore. These tactics do you no good. Have done and come willingly as you promised.'

His arms dragged her close and his lips came down fiercely on her mouth. She tried to struggle, but he was too strong. His damp lips moved across her neck and down to her breasts. She shuddered and his eyes rose. He laughed. 'Fight as you will, my lady. You'll call me master before the night is out.'

He swept her into his arms and carried her into the next room, flinging her down on to the bed. Then his fingers hooked into the flimsy gown and with a hiss the silk tore away, leaving her breasts bare. His hands moved over her body. She closed her eyes to shut out the intensity of his lewd stare, then he was beside her on the bed, his arms holding her in a vice-like grip as he sought her mouth again.

CHAPTER TWELVE

ALYCE tore her mouth away from Count Hubert's and tried to push him from her.

'My lord—give me leave—I—I am going to be sick.'

He reared up on his elbows, glaring at her suspiciously, but one look at her deathly-white face convinced him of the sincerity of her words. He rolled over on to his back. 'There's a bucket in the corner. Get it over quickly. Too much wine, you stupid wench! I should have known better than to indulge you. Be quick about it.'

He watched her balefully as she stumbled from the bed and staggered across the floor to sink weakly beside the bucket. Her head was spinning, her stomach churning, and a fierce band of heat gripping her brow made her moan in anguish as she made good her promise. She heard the Count muttering in frustration but nothing mattered any more, she felt too ill to care.

Gradually the pain in her stomach lessened, and her head became clearer. Perspiration turned cold and she began to shudder uncontrollably, wanting nothing more than to be tucked into a warm bed with only Meg to attend her. But Count Hubert was waiting. He would not brook more delay.

She clutched the rags of her gown closer, but there was no warmth in them. He noticed her shivering.

'Come back to bed, my lady. I'll have you warm in no time.'

'A moment, my lord.' Alyce rose from her knees, steadying herself on the chest beneath the window, then moved slowly towards a washstand. A jug of water stood beside the basin.

With trembling hands she poured a measure into a goblet and drank deeply, trying to rid herself of the taste of stale wine. She damped the end of a towel and wiped her face and neck, pushing back the hair that clung to her temples. She was recovering rapidly but moved slowly, as if to convince Count Hubert of her weakness.

The bed-straps creaked and there was a thud as de Louches' heels hit the floor. She heard the heavy tread approaching, then her shoulder was grasped. He spun her round to face him.

'Your colour is back. You're well enough. So now to bed, my lady, to finish what we began.'

The hand that gripped her wrist was so tight that she could do nothing to stop from following as he dragged her across the floor. She felt herself lifted and tossed once more on to the bed. He stared down at her for a moment as she pulled up the coverings, then he unfastened his tunic and tossed it aside. She closed her eyes against the gross hairiness of his heavy body, the thick waist and flabby paunch.

A thunderous pounding on the outer door made them both jump.

'My lord! My lord!' a voice called urgently.

'Go away!' roared Count Hubert. 'You heard my orders!'

'My lord! My lord!' the voice repeated. 'You must come!'

Count Hubert flung open the bedroom door as the outer doors burst open. Alyce saw the Sergeant hesitating on the threshold.

'Blood of Christ!' thundered de Louches. 'I'll have your ears for this! Did I not say I was to be undisturbed again this night?'

'Yes, my lord, but——'

'If this is some fool's errand you're on, you'll pay dearly, let me warn you.'

'Yes, my lord, but the castle is on fire.'

'Spine of God! What's that you say?'

'The castle, my lord. The drawbridge is aflame and the stables have gone up like a tinderbox. We've freed the horses, but they're panicking and going mad in the bailey, trampling any who go near. We can't get to the well for them.'

The crash of falling timbers added weight to his words, and Count Hubert bent and snatched up his tunic from the floor.

'How did it start, man? Tell me that,' he asked as he struggled into the garment.

'We don't know, my lord. Everything burst into flames at the same moment.'

Count Hubert sat heavily on the bed and pulled on his boots. Alyce stayed quite still, hardly able to believe she had been reprieved at the last moment.

'Get back to your duties, man,' ground out de Louches. 'I will follow.'

The Sergeant went swiftly. Count Hubert looked over his shoulder. 'I'll be back, my lady, never fear.' He stamped from the room and she heard his footsteps hurrying along the corridor.

Alyce thrust herself from the bed and ran to a narrow window. Fires were raging in several different areas. One could not have ignited the other, she decided. The castle was too spacious to huddle everything together.

She ran to another window, one that overlooked the drawbridge. The line of fire ran steadily upwards, almost in a straight line, as if the lower parts had all been fired at the same time. Harry? she wondered. Could Harry really have done all this or was it truly accidental? Design or chance—what did it matter—if it kept Count Hubert away?

She gave a gasp as she heard footsteps flying along the corridor. Surely not the Count back already? But it was Meg who came racing into the room. She skidded to a halt, her eyes searching.

Alyce ran from the bedroom. 'Meg! Meg! I'm here. What happened?'

The girl's eyes lighted on the silk cloak and she snatched it up. 'Quickly, my lady. Put this on and come with me.'

Alyce swirled the cloak about herself and fastened the clasp. 'Oh, Meg! Was it Harry? I'd given up hope.'

'Yes, my lady. He stole some brandy from the cellar and took it to the guardhouse. He told them the Count had sent it for them to drink to his success with you. They didn't need telling twice, but it took a while for them to get drunk.'

They were hurrying along the corridor towards the steps leading to the kitchens on the lower floor.

'Then Harry soaked rags from another barrel of brandy and stuffed them under the drawbridge along with handfuls of dry straw,' went on Meg.

'Where are we going now?'

'To the stable area. Harry will try to get a horse saddled, then you can get away in the confusion and fetch help. At least you will be safe from the Count if you can reach your own castle.'

As they arrived at the head of the stairs they heard footsteps pounding up them.

'Quick, Meg! Into this alcove.' Alyce dragged the girl into the shadows.

Two soldiers came into view. 'All the jugs you can find, my lord said. Go you into the solar while I fetch that bucket from my lord's chamber.'

'Don't disturb the lady,' one laughed. The other echoed his laughter.

'If she were not the Count's property I should disturb her with pleasure, but I have need of my ears, so I'll do no more than look at her, more's the pity.'

They disappeared into separate rooms as a voice called up the stairs. 'Be quick with the buckets. I'm waiting.'

Meg looked at Alyce with dismay. 'We can't go down now, and when the soldiers come back they'll see us.'

'The turret room, Meg. We must run quickly before the soldiers come out of the rooms. There's no other way to go.'

Meg picked up her skirts and ran like a hare after Alyce. They were barely in time to reach the steps before hearing the soldiers rejoin each other.

'Did you see her?' asked one.

'No. She's under the bedclothes, likely. The bed was all tumbled about.'

Alyce and Meg hugged the wall in silence as the voices receded.

'Shall we try again, Meg?'

'We're too late, my lady. They'll recognise you. They'll be in and out of the kitchens fetching pans and buckets. Somebody would tell the Count.'

'Then we've only the battlements left for choice.'

They made their way swiftly. The night sky was lit with a fierce radiance as smoke and flames shot upwards. The crack and crash of burning wood was loud in their ears. The turret room door stood ajar.

'Meg! Where are the others?' Alyce asked in alarm.

'Quite safe, my lady. When the fires started, Harry ran up to tell the Sergeant he should inform the Count at once. The Sergeant agreed and then he said he'd go straight down to the bailey to help with the horses afterwards. When he'd gone, Harry unbolted the door. We all crept down the steps and waited until the Count left his chamber. Then I came for you while Harry took the others down the back way through the kitchens. Just outside is the stone-walled herb store that bolts from the inside. They'll all be in there by now and quite safe. No one could get in without a battering-ram.'

'Thank God,' breathed Alyce. 'They might have chance to escape if the drawbridge is burned right away.'

Meg peered over the battlements. 'If we can't find a rope we might have to jump for it, my lady. We're trapped up here.'

Alyce's laugh was tremulous. 'I would welcome even that to escape the Count.'

'Were—were we in time, my lady?' asked Meg, hesitantly.

'Only just, Meg. I drank so much wine I was sick, and that delayed the Count for a while. I swear I shall not touch wine again in my life. I never felt so ill.'

Meg looked over her shoulder. 'Harry will be wondering where we are. If they get the fire under control, it might be too late to escape. Perhaps we should jump now.'

'Wait, Meg.' Alyce was staring out over the battlement wall. 'Meg! Do you see torchlight?'

Meg looked. 'This fire must be lighting the whole countryside. Perhaps the other lords have seen it.'

'And are coming to help? Oh, Meg! Is it possible? Could my father be bringing men to help fight the fire?'

The two girls stared at each other with dawning hope.

'Look, Meg, they're coming from the direction of the river. It *must* be them!'

'And if the Count sees them he'll come searching for you, to hide you away until they've gone.'

The torches were nearer. She saw their reflections in the water as they crossed the river bridge. Could she hear the jingle of harness, or was it only imagination? The roar of the fire was so much that she could not be sure.

But now the horses were visible, and in the glare of the fire she saw the glint of eight chainmailed figures bent forward over the saddles. Sparks of light raised a glitter on sword and shield. They were coming in fast.

Alyce sprang to life. 'The sheets, Meg! The white bedsheets! If we attract their attention they'll see us full well in this glare.'

They raced to the turret room, flinging aside blankets and

grasping the bedsheets, then back to the battlement wall. The horsemen were almost at the blazing drawbridge. They reined in as great baulks of timber parted and fell hissing into the moat. Smoke and steam rose in a cloud as Alyce flung the sheet over the wall and Meg took the other end.

They flapped the sheet wildly, screaming for help. The smoke thinned as part of the drawbridge settled in the water. What remained had dropped from the chains and lay spanning the moat, its edges rimmed with shooting flames. Alyce screamed, again and again. Surely they must hear! Was her father there? Her eyes were watering with the smoke and she blinked quickly to clear her vision.

'Father!' she screamed. 'It's Alyce. For the love of God, hear me!'

The flames seemed to be lessening. Was Count Hubert now in control? Would he turn away the helpers? She could not let that happen.

'Help me! Help me!' she cried despairingly, and let drop the end of the sheet. It billowed widely in an uprush of smoke. A face looked up, and eyes caught by the movement suddenly searched the battlements. Alyce choked in mid-scream, staring down. The face that stared back was marred by a scar that ran across the cheek. The lips moved, but she could hear nothing.

'Roger!' she called, but the man was already moving. She saw the spurs go in, then the horse charged the narrow path of crackling wood, gathered itself together and rose like an arrow from a longbow. Through smoke and falling debris it hurtled forward between the watchtowers to disappear from her view.

Alyce blinked back the sudden rush of tears and clung to Meg. 'Oh, Meg! I think we are saved. It's Sir Roger. He won't let Count Hubert stop him, I know.'

They heard the sound of voices and running footsteps. Alyce stared expectantly at the steps, her heart full of longing and joy at this relief. Several people were coming, it seemed, but the voices were harsh and muffled by the noise.

The first face she saw chilled the rising happiness. She gasped and fell back to the wall. Count Hubert, with drawn sword, was advancing on her, his eyes wild in his smoke-streaked face. Behind him came two soldiers bearing the insignia of de Louches on their livery.

They spread out, one on each side of the stairhead. Count Hubert faced the steps, his sword held ready.

Alyce heard the footsteps mounting and froze with horror. 'Go back!' she screamed. 'Go back! They're waiting to kill you, Sir Roger.'

The footsteps halted. 'How many?' asked a calm voice.

'Two—and de Louches.'

'Is that all?' There was a mocking note in the voice.

'You cannot fight three. Save yourself and go back, I beg of you!'

'Are you wedded to him, my lady?'

'No, nor am I anything else yet. But I will become whatever he wants if it will save your life. Please do as I ask, for he'll show you no mercy.'

There was a short silence. 'Come on, de Boveney,' jeered Count Hubert. 'Face the lady and tell her your life is more precious than her love. Then get you gone from here. I promise you safe conduct to the gates, nothing more.'

There was no answer.

'Why so silent, Sir Knight?' asked de Louches. 'Do you wait for an invitation to the wedding? But that comes second to what I have in store for my lady.'

De Louches frowned as the silence continued. He motioned to one of his soldiers. The man turned to the steps and looked down. He gave a choking gasp then slumped to the ground, blood pouring from a chest wound. The other soldier leapt back as de Boveney took the steps at a run.

LADY OF STARLIGHT 149

The speed of his move took the Count by surprise. He gaped stupidly at the tall young knight whose sword still dripped with blood.

'Kill him!' he cried chokingly, and the second soldier flung himself forward. Alyce saw the hard dark face break into a half-smile as he fended off the soldier's blade with an almost contemptuous skill. The smile drew the scar up towards the eye corner, giving the knight a faintly piratical look.

The soldier began to breathe heavily, his sword no match for the darting blade of de Boveney. He was overweight and coarse-featured. It did not need Meg's muttered encouragement of the knight to know that she held the soldier in disgust as one of the more brutal men-at-arms.

The contest was soon over. The knight was wise enough to avoid turning his back on de Louches, who moved from side to side seeking an opening. The flailing blade of the soldier spun from his hand as de Boveney delivered the fatal thrust. He collapsed suddenly like a stringless puppet doll, his lifeless eyes staring up into the red sky.

And Roger was hardly out of breath, Alyce thought admiringly, her heart full of love.

'My lord?' said the knight on a question. 'Will you now try your skill? You have no one left to do your fighting.' As the Count hesitated, the mocking voice went on. 'Is the lady not prize enough to risk your blade against mine?'

De Louches brought up his sword slowly, reddening at the words. He had not fought in single combat for many years, preferring his soldiers to do it for him. Although much younger than the King and perhaps a bare ten years older than de Boveney, wine and loose living had blurred and coarsened the once taut body.

The knight threw a quick glance at Alyce. 'Whatever the outcome, my lady, you are safe. I rode ahead with my men when we saw the fire, but your father follows. He'll be here within the half-hour. My men know of your presence and will make him aware of it too.' He looked at de Louches, his lips curving in amusement. 'Why so silent, Count Hubert? Do you wait for an invitation?'

A vein throbbed in de Louches' forehead. Perspiration sheened his face. Before he could move, there was the sound of running footsteps rising swiftly to them. Four men burst into view, three of them wearing the de Louches insignia. The fourth was Harry.

Alyce gasped in horror as she saw the Sergeant with drawn blade. Harry stood behind him, his hand on the hilt of a dagger. His eyes met de Boveney's in recognition.

'My weapon, such as it is, is at your service, sir.' He moved swiftly to ally himself with the knight.

De Louches gazed triumphantly at de Boveney. 'None left, eh? You are mistaken. Even with the scullion yonder, you are outnumbered.'

'But he was a soldier, as you well know, and I am proud to accept his offer.'

'Go to it, Sergeant,' commanded the Count. 'Cut down this insolent knight and that traitorous scullion. You will be well rewarded.'

Alyce watched the Sergeant, her hands clasped in silent entreaty, her eyes huge with pleading. She willed him to look at her, but his eyes were on the Count; his stare was cold, and loathing grew on his face.

'No reward will count higher with me than to see you put where you belong. Your place is on the dungheap with the bones of those you sent before. I've had enough of your cruelty. My sword is for the knight—if he will accept it.'

'Gladly, Sergeant. So now we are three against three, de Louches. Shall we make a start, or do you wait for more support?'

The two soldiers exchanged swift glances. They abruptly sheathed their swords. 'I have no stomach to fight de Louches' battles any more,' said one.

'Nor I,' added his companion. 'I am a soldier, not an assassin.'

'What now, lord Count?' asked the mocking voice. 'It seems we are left in sole charge of the field. Shall we then engage in mortal combat?'

De Louches glared round at his reluctant soldiers. 'Obey my orders or you will suffer for it! I'll have you all flayed alive and cut into pieces for the dogs.'

'You will not have time for that diversion, my lord,' the knight commented, 'for your life will end before the night is over. Guard the steps, Sergeant, if your word holds good. I claim the right of sole combat with the Count.'

'Yes, sir.' The Sergeant moved smartly to the stairhead. He was joined by the two soldiers. Harry moved over to Meg.

'Keep well back, love,' he murmured. 'Stand clear, my lady. The Count may swing wild.'

De Boveney saluted the Count, then took his stance. De Louches' look was ugly as it rested on his own men, then he turned to de Boveney. 'I killed men before you were breeched,' he said menacingly. 'I'll spit you like a capon.'

The scar curved as the knight smiled. He was unmoved by the threats. 'But that was before you took up the ways of the swine, my lord. Far better you had stayed a swineherd as I imagine your father was. I'm told your title was handed you only after the conquest of England.' He shook his head sadly. 'Even a King is not immune to misjudgment. But I will right that fault in his name.'

'Insolent dog!' roared de Louches, and lunged.

His opponent had the advantage of a slim, lithe body that moved swiftly to avoid the outstretched blade. Even in her terror that he might be killed, Alyce could not help but admire the fleetness of foot. De Louches was like a lumbering ox in comparison but still a dangerous foe at close quarters. If Roger should be hurt, the Count would not hesitate to run him through without mercy, she knew.

But the knight was well-trained. He avoided with dexterity the crushing blows de Louches swung at him. He even laughed, infuriating the Count, as he said, 'You use your sword like a battleaxe, my lord, or a peasant out tree-felling. Is that the way you urged your pigs?'

Count Hubert's face was dark red and sweat poured down his cheeks. His blade met air each time he lunged or swung. Thick veins stood out on his forehead and his body moved slower as he turned to face the darting blade that seemed to come from all directions. His breathing was laboured but he was far from finished. He paused, gasping, his eyes on the knight. A swift flashing lunge caught the left sleeve of his opponent. It ripped to the shoulder, leaving a slight wound on de Boveney's arm.

Alyce clapped a hand to her mouth to still a cry.

'First blood to me, de Boveney,' roared Count Hubert triumphantly, and tried to follow up his success by hurling himself bodily at the knight in an attempt to overpower him by sheer weight.

But the wound was too slight to slow down his opponent. His blade rose swiftly and the point disappeared, to appear again as a crimson-stained point, spitting de Louches neatly through the chest.

The Count fell backwards, crashing heavily to the ground. He lay blank-eyed, motionless, the de Boveney blade quivering upright in his chest.

Alyce stared, fascinated, at the hilt and crosspiece, the blood bubbling and surging from the point of entry. The gross body lay still, colour draining from the face. She waited, but no one spoke. It was as if they all expected him to rise and fight on. It seemed unbelievable that the terrible Count Hubert was dead.

The Sergeant was the first to move. He crossed to the body and laid a finger on the neck, then looked up at Alyce. He nodded.

'Dead, my lady, by God's grace and the skill of the knight.' He glanced over at the victor. 'This is a happy day for us, sir. I will go below and pass on the tidings.' He jerked his head at the two soldiers and they moved down the steps together.

'Come, Meg,' said Harry, 'we can now release my lady's servants from the herb store. I see Earl Robert's party approaching. We must give him the news.'

Alyce turned her gaze from the distant figures nearing the river bridge and found the knight regarding her keenly as he leaned against the battlement wall. She crossed to him swiftly, looking up into the dark face with anxiety. His cheeks were thinner, the eyes more intense, but that was only to be expected after long weeks of soldiering in harsh weather.

'I have dreamed of this moment for so long,' she said, tears glistening on her eyelashes. 'I thought never to see you again.'

'Nor I you, my lady. If it had not been for the fire, we would never have known you were here and not in Denmark. A lucky chance indeed.'

'Not luck, sir, for it was executed by Meg's husband in a bid to help us escape.'

He was trying, one-handed, to rip the sleeve from his shirt. She took it from him and tore it into strips. 'Let me bind up your wound. I have no herbs, but this cloth will hold the bleeding.' She pushed back her cloak and concentrated on the task. 'I am so glad you killed him. I could not have borne any more of his treatment. I was prepared to leap into the moat before submitting further.'

She glanced down and suddenly became aware of her gaping bodice. Her fingers fluttered over the tattered silk. 'Oh, I forgot——' she began, then found her hands gripped in a strong clasp. Her gaze flew up. She started to tremble, her self-control deserting her.

'I've tried so hard to be brave,' she whispered, 'but I am

going to cry. I cannot help it, I am so happy to be with you again, my love. Forgive me——'

His arms encircled her comfortingly. She laid her cheek on his chest like a tired child and let the tears fall.

'Forgive you? For being brave and defying that monster?' His voice deepened with emotion. 'We had sent to the Danes and were awaiting a reply.' His hands tightened. 'I would kill the Count ten times over to save you. God's love—if only I'd known sooner where you were, I would have stormed the castle to come to you. I never realised how much you meant to me until we heard you were taken.'

She drew back her head, looking into his eyes. 'It is not too late if you love me still. I thought only of you while we lay a week in these dungeons——'

He stared. 'God's teeth! He kept you in the dungeons?'

She nodded. 'It was only when he threatened to torture my servants that I consented to—to his demands. Even so, I bargained for two days' grace. But for the fire, I should by now have been his mistress.'

'My poor child.' His arms tightened about her slim shoulders.

With a return of her old spirit, Alyce glanced up, smiling. 'Child I am not! How can you say that, after all I have been through?'

He met her eyes in a long smiling glance and his voice was husky as he said on a helpless half-laugh, 'How can I indeed, with the evidence in front of my eyes?'

His fingers moved over her breasts caressingly, as he drew the torn silk over them, then his hand rose to take her chin in a tender clasp. 'You are far and away the bravest, most beautiful, most desirable lady of my acquaintance. I shall not rest until I have you tied to my side by marriage vows. Will you marry me, Alyce?'

Her hands crept up to rest on his chest. 'Need you ask? Of course I will. I have always loved you, Roger.'

He held back for a moment, cupping her face in his hands as his eyes looked deep into hers. There was doubt in his gaze, a reluctance to accept her admission.

'What do you know of love, Alyce? A few kisses in the stables, a tender handclasp? You are young—I should not take advantage of that.' He stared down, broodingly. 'I am not the man you think—not the romantic hero of adventure, nor of your young girl's dreams. Perhaps it is ill of me to talk of love and seek to bind you. There have been women in my life, but never a one who clutched my heart as you have done.'

'I may be young in years, my lord, but I have learned much this past week. I know that marriage is not of sighs and flattering words. It is a coming together in love, of body and mind. The Count's nearness revolted me, but when you lay your hand on me I delight in your touch. Perhaps I was a child when we last met, but now I know a woman's needs. My heart and body are yours. I surrender them willingly. Do you wish to deny what is yours by conquest?'

His hands slid to her shoulders. As if the words were forced from him, he said on a half-laugh, half-groan, 'I cannot deny you or myself. I may be doing you a great wrong, but you have held my heart and mind since we last met. I will fight the world to keep you.'

She found herself held fast, locked in an embrace as his mouth came down fiercely. His chainmail pressed into her breasts but she did not feel the discomfort as her lips answered his. They stood for a long moment, tightly pressed together, oblivious to the sound of galloping hooves and loud voices from below.

At last he released her reluctantly and she drew her fingers gently across the scar, tracing its passage from cheekbone to eye corner.

'Does my scar disgust you, my heart?'

She shook her head. 'I love you the more because of it. You

earned it in honour. And this——' her gaze went to the body of de Louches. 'This too—for my sake.'

'Then and now—for your sake only. Let it count in my favour, sweetheart, whatever befalls.'

'I will carry both memories to my grave.'

He laughed softly, his doubts gone. 'Talk not of graves, my heart. We have not yet lived in love. But soon—when this winter of waiting is over—I will come to you and claim what is mine by love and conquest. None shall defy or deny me, Alyce, I swear by the Holy relics.'

She had time only to whisper, 'I will be waiting, my dearest lord,' before Meg came running into view.

CHAPTER
THIRTEEN

'My lady—Sir Roger—forgive me, but Earl Robert is on his way up. He must not see his daughter so attired in the presence of his soldiers. Come, we must get you into that tunic again, my lady, before he reaches this place.'

'She is right, Alyce,' put in de Boveney. 'Go quickly. I will not have the rough soldiery gazing upon your beauty.' His smiling glance was full of sudden amusement. 'That sight is strictly reserved for lovers and physicians.'

Alyce giggled, light-headed with happiness. 'Will I see you again when I am more suitably clad?'

'I think not. I was on urgent business for the King when all this happened. I must make up for lost time. But Alyce——' he drew her close. 'Hold this secret in your heart until I have seen the King.' He kissed her swiftly and turned, running lightly down the steps, affixing his helm as he went.

Alyce fled to the turret room. Was it only a few hours since she left it, sick with foreboding at what she was to endure? She stared round the room. It was like coming home after sentence had been lifted. Meg was hurrying her out of the silk dress, lifting the tunic to fling over her head. Alyce took the Count's gold chain and hurled it into a corner. She would keep nothing he had touched.

Meg was trying to bring order to her hair when Alyce heard her father's voice. She sprang up and ran out on to the battlements, throwing herself into Earl Robert's arms. He held her tightly and she felt a shudder run through him.

'Alyce, Alyce, my dearest child,' he murmured into her hair. 'How could the Count be so base? I thought him a friend and dismissed the tales they told. Forgive me, Alyce, for ever doubting you.'

He held her away from him, his eyes searching her face. 'You are thin and pale. You have suffered much. If de Louches were not already dead—by de Boveney's hand, they tell me, though I could scarce recognise him in the smoke below—I would kill him myself for this treatment. God's bones! The man must have been deranged to plan such harsh revenge.'

'Unused to opposition, Father, but let us not talk of him. Take me home, I beg of you.' To her own surprise, the tears began to fall as reaction set in.

Meg swept a blanket about her trembling figure and Earl Robert, with an exclamation of distress, picked her up, cradling her close to his chest.

Alyce remembered her companions. 'Meg,' she called, over his shoulder, 'bring them all. Harry too.'

'Of course, my lady. They'll be as glad to quit this place as you are.'

Earl Robert hurried down the steps through the swirling smoke, calling his men to bring up his horse. Alyce looked back once as they galloped away. The de Louches castle was slowly being destroyed. No one cared enough now to check the fire. The body of Count Hubert would disintegrate in the flames, along with his despotic rule.

Baulks of timber had been hastily laid across the moat; castle servants ran back and forth, saving what they could for their own use. The reign of de Louches was over. By tomorrow night the castle would stand a ruined shell, the Count unmourned by any, save perhaps a few low-born men-at-arms and kitchen sluts.

When they reached the Beaumont castle, Earl Robert strode through the hall and straight upstairs with Alyce still in his arms. His hands were gentle as he helped her from the tunic and into her own bed, drawing up the bearskin cover.

Her body relaxed on the goose-feather mattress and she smiled into his anxious face.

'I need nothing but sleep, Father. Truly, I have suffered no lasting harm. I am still a maid, and for that reason I hope you will welcome my friends when they come with Meg.'

'What friends are these, my love?'

'Apart from Meg's husband who was tied in service to de Louches, you should know them all. They are from your own kitchens. They stood by me in such loyalty that I can never repay my debt to them.'

'Then I, too, am in their debt. But sleep now, my dear, and we will discuss their reward tomorrow when you are rested.'

The last thing Alyce saw was his gentle smile and then she fell asleep. For ten hours she slept, barely stirring. It was as if her body and mind had ceased to function, to allow a healing, dreamless oblivion to rejuvenate her completely.

Her eyes opened slowly. There was nothing to alarm her. Light streamed through the window, she was warm and refreshed and no terror lay in store. Her fingers moved over the bearskin; it was reassuringly real. Then Meg came smiling to her side and she knew she was back where she had started.

'My lord Earl asked to be notified immediately you woke, my lady,' she said, 'but first you must drink this milk I have heated. Ranulf is here, too, with fresh-baked rolls.'

Alyce looked at her page as he knelt and offered the plate. 'It's good to see you, Ranulf.' Apart from a small bandage on his ear, he seemed quite cheerful as he gave her a little smile.

'I will wash and dress before I see my father, Meg. Has everyone arrived back safely? Harry too?'

'Yes, my lady. The lord Earl greeted us most graciously. When he has talked to you, he will see us all again, he said. My lady—do you think he would take Harry into his service now that the Count is dead? Harry is a good soldier and must find a new master, but perhaps my lord Earl will not want one who has served Count Hubert.'

'Don't worry, Meg. When I tell my father that Harry fired the castle and save me from dishonour, you may be sure there will be a place for him here.'

Earl Robert arrived as Alyce finished dressing. He looked intently at her as Meg curtsied and left them alone.

'You look rested, my dear, but still too thin and pale.'

Alyce smiled. 'Give me time, Father! A few days and I shall be back to normal.'

He nodded and took her arm. 'Let us go up to the solar and sit in comfort, then you may tell me all that has happened, if it will not distress you.'

They sat one on each side of a blazing fire, and Alyce recounted every detail of the events that followed the Earl's departure for Pevensey Bay. She omitted only the final scene in Roger's arms, in deference to her father's rigid code of behaviour. His horror and anger grew until he could no longer sit still, but fell to pacing the floor.

'I am almost sorry he is dead,' Earl Robert said, savagely. 'I would have given much to kill the swine myself. May he be paying tenfold in hell for his villainy, for he must surely be there at this moment. It is no wonder his men finally turned against him.'

'Poor Edith,' Alyce said. 'She paid with her life for recognising one of the so-called Danes.'

'But you avenged her before they overpowered you.' He stood, looking down at her proudly. 'You are a true Beaumont, my love, even to holding off de Louches for two days. The poor fool discounted your wits and suffered for it, thank God.'

'It's all over now, Father, but I would like to talk to you of those who helped me.'

'Yes, indeed. They shall be well rewarded. What can I do for them?'

'They are good people, Father. What they did was done proudly for our sake.'

'I can offer them higher positions, Alyce. This cook, Wilfred, seems a man of intelligence. He would make a good chief steward in place of the one murdered by de Louches. We will give him the lad, Edgar, to train as he sees fit, perhaps as a serving page. The girls I will leave to you, my love, for they are more in your province.'

'And will you take Meg's husband into your service, Father? Please do.'

'Indeed I will. A man of such resource should be at least a Sergeant. De Louches killed my last one, along with several good men.'

'And Father,' said Alyce, remembering, 'there was a Sergeant in the Count's service who was sympathetic towards me, and turned on the Count in the end. May I ask Harry to bring him to you?'

Earl Robert laughed. 'All right, my dear, but I warn you, I have no intention of employing the whole of de Louches' motley crowd! I will see your Sergeant and put him to the test myself, but I want none of his men-at-arms.'

'No, Father. There is no one else in my mind.'

Before dinner that night she saw Wilfred. She hardly recognised the erect, grey-haired man as the one she had first met in the dungeons. He wore the livery of head steward proudly. She inspected the tables, as was her custom, and greeted him in friendly fashion.

'Well, Wilfred. Does this position please you, my friend?'

He bowed. 'It pleases me greatly, my lady. I have always wanted the chance to rise. You and my lord Earl will be satisfied, I promise.'

'And can you find something suitable for Edgar?'

'Yes, my lady. He is not lacking in wits, and I will teach him to serve at table. He is overjoyed to think he is no longer a scullion.'

'And the girls, Wilfred? What can I do for them?'

'They have asked if they may work in the dairy if it pleases you, my lady.'

'Of course. You may tell them so.'

'Thank you, my lady.' He smiled. 'It is good to be home.' The words were plainly said but uttered with such feeling that Alyce responded warmly.

'It is indeed, Wilfred. I could not have borne it without the support of you all. None of you shall ever lack while the Beaumonts live,' she promised.

When Alyce retired for the night, she found Meg in a state of bubbling excitement. 'Oh, my lady,' she said, 'my lord Earl has taken Harry into his service. He is to be a Sergeant as soon as he has proved himself. We are to have the old Sergeant's quarters to live in.'

'I am pleased for you, Meg. You will be able to start your married life now.'

Meg blushed. 'Yes, my lady. I—I hope your own happiness is not long delayed.'

'I, too, Meg, but we must wait for the King's convenience.'

Towards the end of the year, news arrived dispelling all fear of invasion. The Danes had disbanded their armies. When the King was convinced of the truth of this information, he allowed the greater part of his army to return home, retaining only a small number. He spent Christmas at Gloucester, where he held court for five days, attending afterwards a three-day synod held by the Archbishop and the clergy. Three of his chaplains were elected to the bishoprics of London, Norfolk and Cheshire. With the coming of peace and the ending of the Christmas festivities of 1085, William returned to his grand scheme, the great survey of England.

Winter passed into Spring, and Alyce celebrated her seventeenth birthday. She noted with satisfaction that her height had increased by two whole inches. Although still slender, her body had regained the ground it had lost under the Count's treatment. Her skin bloomed with health, her hair shone silkily, and her breasts were firm and rounded, accentuating her tiny waist.

She longed for Roger's return, but attached as he was to the King's court, she realised he must follow his liege lord to Normandy, to Wales or to Scotland, wheresoever his sovereign went.

As the days grew warmer, Earl Robert received news that the King was to spend Easter at Winchester. He had a matter of the heart to arrange, he wrote, and desired his old comrade-in-arms, Robert de Beaumont, to attend on him in this matter.

Alyce stood before her father, listening as he read the letter aloud. In the glow from the fire in the great hearth her face became rosy, and her eyes gleamed like amber jewels. It was almost a year since the visit of the King, but her confidence in him had never waned. Her heart beat fast as she thought of that night on the de Louches battlements, the strength of Roger's arms and the fierceness of his kisses.

'His Majesty,' went on her father, 'mentions too that Lord de Boveney has been summoned to attend.'

Alyce nodded. She had expected that. Roger had spoken to the King, and here was the summons at last.

Earl Robert smiled up into the glowing face. 'Well, daughter! The King has now the time to redeem his promise. You are still of the same mind, my dear, as when we talked after sending the Count about his business?' His voice became teasing. 'The bearskin on your bed—it brings you pleasant dreams of the knight who won it for you?'

Alyce blushed. 'Yes, Father.'

He was satisfied, and preparations began for his visit to Winchester. A secretary was to accompany him, together with quills and parchments to draw up the marriage contract. Earl Robert's secretary had been closeted with his master for hours, penning details of the dowry. The settlements were to be finalised when both parties met in Winchester.

It was quiet after her father had gone, but not uneventful. Merchants carrying rolls of silk and fine cotton came up to the castle and girls were hired to put together my lady's bride-clothes. English women as well as Norman were skilled in embroidery. Shoemakers came and went, merchants bearing fine furs, pedlars with ribbons and exotic perfumes from Byzantium thronged the courtyard daily.

With the milder weather, Alyce and Meg took their stitching into the sweet-scented herb garden where honeysuckle had begun to riot amongst the shrubs by the wall. Tiny spring flowers peeped over their leaves as Alyce sat stitching and dreaming of a white stallion appearing atop the hills with the banner of de Boveney flying above in the sunshine.

She thought of the King who always wore his crown in public at the Easter, Ascension and Christmas feasts, and was attended by the entire baronage. She hoped her father would bring her news of Roger himself and not just of the settlements necessary to a betrothal. Perhaps he might bring a letter or a gift. In that event she must reply with a gift. A linen shirt, she mused, or an embroidered belt? Perhaps a fur-trimmed mantle. Whatever it was to be it must be made by her alone and stitched with love.

The weeks passed and at last a messenger came to tell her that Earl Robert was preparing for his return. The King had left Winchester to journey to Westminster. He was due there on Whit Sunday for the knighting of his son Henry.

Alyce questioned the messenger eagerly, but he knew little except that the King's procession through the town had been a glittering affair with all the nobles in their armour and every horse dressed in jewelled trappings. The people had cheered the King, magnificent in purple and gold, and had

LADY OF STARLIGHT 165

stared in awe at the array of silken banners and the lines of armed men. And at the hunt later, although the King was not a young man, he had amazed everyone by his strength in letting fly an arrow at full gallop from a bow that many younger men could not even bend. And, the messenger said in admiration, he had brought down a wild boar with that one shot.

Alyce tried to question him more particularly, but as a groom he knew little beyond horses and squires. She dismissed him kindly, sending him to the kitchens to receive food and drink.

Two days later her father returned. She and Meg were in the herb garden. The weather had stayed mild, and Alyce was working on a velvet mantle. The colour was deep blue and she planned to line it with grey silk and border it with marten fur. Roger would look superb in it. Perhaps with neck fastenings of silver cord and embroidered—— She stopped suddenly and raised her head. The sound of a horn wound from the distant hills, and through the stillness of the afternoon her ears picked up the faintest clop of hoofbeats. She placed the mantle carefully on the bench and looked at Meg.

'My lord Earl comes?' asked her maid.

'It must be him,' said Alyce, her heart beginning to race. 'I'll go up to the turret and look across the valley.'

She went into the keep slowly but once out of sight of the servants, lifted her skirts and ran up the stairs. She flew across the battlements and gripped the stonework, narrowing her eyes against the sun. The gorse, golden-yellow, flowed over the heath, and the bushes clinging to the hillside displayed their new shoots of pale green. A pheasant rose from the ground with a startled cry and fled into the thicket.

At the same moment Alyce saw the glitter of speartips. The gonfalon of the Beaumonts flew high in the cloudless sky as the standard-bearer crested the hill. Beneath the banner Alyce recognised her father, tall in the saddle of his black destrier. Soon she would know if she was betrothed or not. There seemed no reason for any hitch, and yet her heart beat with long measured thuds as her hands clasped themselves tightly together.

The company of men-at-arms came steadily closer until they were within clear view of the gate. She heard the rattle of chains and the drawbridge thumped down. Hens screeched and voices rose in the bailey. The stables were thrown open, grooms and servants appeared to greet the travellers and Alyce herself turned from her contemplation, realising that until her father had eaten and rested, nothing would be discussed. She had time to speak to Wilfred and learn that he had anticipated this moment. Baked meats were even now nearing perfection, and my lord's favourite wine was being brought from the cellar.

Alyce thanked him and made her way into the courtyard as Earl Robert dismounted and stretched. He looked tired and there were dark stains under his eyes. She went forward and he smiled, drawing her to him to drop a kiss on her brow.

'God's bones, but I'm weary, daughter. The Old Wolf has lost none of his cunning; he outruns us all in the hunt, and still looks as fresh as a fledgling hawk at the end of the day.' He put a hand under her chin. 'All is well, child, but let me throw off this harness and eat. We've ridden since daybreak and the horses are blown too.'

They went into the castle and the grooms led away the horses. Earl Robert's squire unbuckled the sword belt and began to strip the chainmail off his master. Ranulf appeared with wine and the Earl drained a goblet before going upstairs, where his body servant waited with hot water.

Alyce went to her room, determined to be patient. Meg had brought in the mantle; it lay on the bed carefully folded. Alyce ran her fingers over the velvet gently, picturing it swinging with careless grace from the shoulders of the tall knight who had conquered her heart.

A tap on the door revealed Ranulf, reporting that the lord Earl was changed and the meat ready to be served. Alyce went down quickly to rejoin her father in the hall. An appetising smell of roast duck and loin of pork hung in the air as she took her place at the table. Earl Robert looked more relaxed in his long loose tunic and he attacked his meal with the fervour of a starving man. His knights were with him, all discussing the King's visit to Winchester and his prowess in the field. Alyce listened with interest, knowing that her father would not talk of private business until they were alone.

That moment came at last. The spring sun had deepened towards twilight and spread like a cloth of gold flung across the horizon, violet shadows creeping into every corner. The knights left and the tables were cleared. With his arm about her shoulders, Earl Robert mounted the stone stairway to the solar.

A fire was burning, candles threw soft light across the tapestries and embroidered stool-cushions. Earl Robert let himself down into an armchair and indicated a package placed on a side table.

'Your betrothed sends you gifts, my child. Will you not open them?'

Alyce obeyed and was enchanted by the jewelled slippers and girdles, the sapphire-set silver bracelet and the two-handed goblet which had birds and fawns delicately carved round the bowl.

'They're beautiful, Father. How thoughtful of him.' She moved to a stool and looked up at the Earl. 'Did he seem happy about the betrothal?'

She had to know. In the heat of emotion aroused by a duel to the death, a man might live to regret passionate words.

'Happy? He was not, of course, present at our discussions, but His Majesty told me he never saw a man more fiercely determined to enter into matrimony.'

Alyce gazed dreamily into the fire. Good fortune had

stayed by her side and the King had stood friend as he had promised.

'I am getting on in years,' her father went on, 'many years older than your dear mother was. I will be glad to see you safely and happily settled. A fine young man he is, daughter, most knightly and brave in battle, the King tells me. And one day you will become a Countess and your sons the lords of Boveney.'

Some faint flicker of disquiet penetrated Alyce's consciousness. She turned to her father, her gaze questioning. 'Lords of Boveney, Father? How is this?'

'How else should it be, child? The old Earl is full of years and the inheritance will soon pass to the present lord. In time, when he leaves this world, though Heaven preserve him for many more years, your betrothed will inherit, for he is the heir.'

Alyce gazed blindly at Earl Robert. His face shimmered, seeming to float disembodied in the shadows. His voice receded like a dim echo in the sudden pounding of blood in her temples. She sought to grasp the reality of his words but her mind was filled with black foreboding. What was he saying? It was some terrible mistake! It had to be.

Her voice came faint and wavering, like a gossamer thread tossed in the breeze. 'Gilbert is the heir, Father. You know he is!'

He stared into her suddenly blanched face, a frown of puzzlement on his brow. 'Yes, my dear, of course I know it. It is to Gilbert you are betrothed.'

CHAPTER FOURTEEN

'To Gilbert, Father? You have betrothed me to Gilbert de Boveney?'

'It was your wish, my child.'

Alyce flung herself up from the stool and stared down at her father. She moved away a few steps, her hands clasped in agitation, then whirled towards him. 'Never, Father! How could you think it? It is Roger de Boveney I love.'

Earl Robert's brow furrowed. He gazed blankly at his daughter. 'When I left to arrange the betrothal, you assured me that that was what you wanted.' His gaze sharpened. 'Have you received Sir Roger in my absence? What has come about to bring this change of heart? You had best tell me the truth, daughter. This is not some small matter with which to trifle when the King is concerned.'

'There have been no callers since you left, Father, and I have not seen Roger.'

She bit her lip, thinking. 'Neither has there been a change of heart. It has always been Roger. I cannot conceive how the King should make such a mistake.'

Earl Robert's voice took on a note of authority. 'Sit down, Alyce, and explain to me how this came about, for I was of the same opinion as the King. It is not often His Majesty takes a personal interest in the affairs of a maid, but he took a fancy to you. What is important at this moment is that he thinks it is Gilbert you wish as husband. He is for Normandy after Westminster, and out of friendship is determined, he said, to honour his royal word to a lady before leaving. How can we now throw such graciousness back in his teeth?'

Alyce sank on to a stool, staring at her father from eyes like dark pools of troubled water. 'You too, Father? I don't understand.'

'Neither do I. The King recalled the incident in the courtyard after the bear hunt. You spoke of Sir Gilbert's remark concerning the securing of a bedcover for you. The King was impressed by your spirited defence of the knight who felled the creature. Few young maids, he said, would have the courage to stand against their King for such a cause. Because of his admiration he resolved to reward you by giving his royal assistance and blessing on your union.'

'I still don't understand.' Alyce pressed her hands against her eyes.

'I asked you myself if you were sure of your own and the knight's affection,' Earl Robert went on sternly. 'You said you had talked with Sir Gilbert in the stables. Were those not the words of one affirming the truth?'

'I talked with him, yes, but of the victory of Sir Roger, who killed the bear!'

'No, daughter, you are mistaken. 'Twas Sir Gilbert.'

'Sir Gilbert? But Roger was clawed in the battle. I dressed his arm.'

'There was a scuffle as I remember, for the bear came silently into our path, but Sir Gilbert's spear took him neatly through the heart.'

In the whirling turmoil of her mind, Alyce strove for recollection. Roger had not actually said he killed the bear, but neither had he denied it. The jewelled dagger had lain at his feet. She had assumed he had won the wager because of it.

But not only that. She recalled Sir Gilbert's mocking laugh and remark to the effect of Roger refusing the spoils of victory when he returned the dagger to his brother. That had convinced her of Roger's feat. And yet, she remembered vaguely, they had spoken over her head. Something about Gilbert accepting—the dagger, she had thought. But if Gilbert had killed the bear—what had the words meant? Nevertheless, her assumption had remained because of Roger's wound.

The fault was her own. Why had she held the secret so close, even from her father? Roger's last words had commanded her to keep silent until he had seen the King. In addition, her own modesty had made her reluctant to recount the passionate scene on the de Louches battlements. How stupid she was! Earl Robert had only seen Roger dimly through the smoke that night, considering him just one of the rescuers rushing to aid a fellow lord. Had she been open and frank about their meeting to her father, this whole disaster could have been averted.

'Father, what can I do?' she asked desperately.

'Nothing, my daughter. It has gone too far. His Majesty, in my presence, sent for the goldsmith to make a set of goblets with both your names engraved upon them. The King's Grace must not be allowed to look foolish. That he will never tolerate, however deep our friendship. But come, Alyce, the knight, Gilbert, is handsome and brave. The King holds him in high regard. You found no fault to his dishonour, did you?'

'N—no, Father.' The memory of that night in the corridor after her encounter with Count Hubert flashed through her mind. He had treated her with harshness and frightened her badly. But to be honest—although her fear of him still lingered—she had provoked him into that swift and merciless retaliation. No one could strike a man such as he and go unpunished.

She remembered his eyes, that bone-chilling look, and shivered. For all his courtier's words before the tournament, she had seen the man behind those flattering words. She, who had pitied the woman he would take for wife, was now to be that wife! How cruel was fate, to deprive her of the gay, laughing Roger and substitute the hard, sharp-tongued, arrogant Gilbert in his place.

Earl Robert touched her hand gently. 'But I see he did not catch your fancy like young Roger?'

She shook her head, staring dully into the fire.

'Then you must learn to love him, my dear, for you are affianced to him.' There was a note of finality in Earl Robert's voice. 'The de Boveneys are a powerful family. We cannot offend both them and the King. The betrothal must stand.'

Alyce left her father in the solar and went into the herb garden where she could think without disturbance. She sank on to the stone bench and rested her chin in her hands. The fragrance of lavender hung in the air and the birds rustled softly in the bushes while a faint lucent glow from the drifting moon silvered the garden. Rosemary and basil gleamed palely from their beds. Stars glinted like diamond studs flung haphazard across a velvet surface. She had always loved starlight, but tonight it reminded her of the blue velvet cloak and the silver-gilt embroidery she had stitched with such love for Roger.

She would never finish it for Gilbert, she vowed. If she was forced to marry him, then he would find her a cold bride with no love in her heart. Her mind quailed. So like the King! Might he take a whip and beat her into submission?

Over the next few days Alyce moved unsmiling about her duties. No one, not even Meg, should see her tears, she vowed inwardly. Several times she caught a sidelong glance from one of the servants, wondering perhaps why she showed none of the excitement of a girl approaching her wedding day. Meg watched her too but said nothing, finding her young mistress unaccountably silent as they completed the bridal clothes, but of the blue velvet cloak she saw no more.

Preparations increased, and at last Alyce's bridal eve arrived. Meg brushed her mistress's long dark hair as she prepared her for bed. Alarmed by the feverish glitter in the reflected eyes she was moved to murmur soothingly, 'You're as tense as a cornered vixen, my lady. Let me mix you a dose of betony to help you sleep. 'Twas gathered on a Thursday when the moon had set in Libra——' She stopped as Alyce met her eyes fiercely.

'Sleep? I shan't sleep tonight.'

'But my lady, a bride must look beautiful——'

'I would that I were as ugly as sin itself,' Alyce retorted stormily. 'Then Sir Gilbert would rue my very existence and flee the country.'

'Hush, my lady,' Meg glanced round quickly. ''Tis no way to talk on your wedding eve. My lord Earl would be angered to hear it.'

'My lord Earl,' Alyce mimicked savagely, 'knows that I do not wish to marry Sir Gilbert. The King wishes it, Sir Gilbert wishes it—God knows why—therefore I must obey.' She swung round to face Meg. 'You are luckier than I, Meg. You made your own choice and were allowed to hold to it.'

'Yes, my lady. We chose each other, but Harry was only a soldier and I was a village girl without dowry. Things are different for noble folk. Your father is Earl Robert and your betrothed is of equal rank with you, besides being the de Boveney heir. These are matters of importance and must be considered.'

'And the bride is of little importance?'

'But my lady, I heard you walked and talked right happily with the gentleman before the tournament that day. A fine young couple you looked. The King's own words too, for I heard it from my lord's body servant.' Her face was full of distress. 'For my part, I have cause to be grateful to any de Boveney for I remember well the market place that day. I thought them both so brave and noble. 'Tis pity you have taken the one so in dislike.'

'But it is all a mistake!' Alyce cried, dropping her head on to her arms. 'I know Sir Roger loves me. He asked me to marry him the night he killed de Louches. Sir Gilbert must have spoken first to the King and secured his promise. The King could not go back on that. He knew nothing of my mistake in supposing Sir Roger killed the bear. When I think how I pleaded for clemency! And the King, all the time, imagining I asked it for Sir Gilbert! Could any girl have such ill-luck!'

Her head came up and she stared darkly at Meg. 'This is my wedding eve and tomorrow I am being married to a man who means nothing to me—nothing at all. I might as well be dead.'

'It is the custom,' Meg murmured uneasily. 'All is arranged, so you must accept it. What other course have you?'

But the mutinous thoughts still lingered after Meg had put her to bed, bidding her sleep well and be of good heart.

Pale fingers of moonlight crept through the slits in the stone wall, touching the motionless figure that sat with arms clasped round her knees. The dark hair fell veil-like about Alyce's hunched shoulders. How could she sleep, knowing that from tomorrow her future would rest in the hands of one who was almost a stranger, a man she neither liked nor trusted. Oh, he would be charming enough in company, but later, when they were ceremoniously bedded then left alone—she trembled at the thought of his fierce mastery when she had struck him. What sweet revenge did he plan? If only he had been Roger. But Roger was not the heir and future lord of Boveney, a fact most pleasing to Earl Robert.

She slipped from the bed, going to the small window and leaning her arms on the cold stone. Sounds floated upwards; the tramp of feet from the gatehouse, the gossiping voices of village girls as they crossed the courtyard from the castle kitchens, a lone merchant urging his donkey towards the hamlet beyond.

If only she had been a cottager's child she might have run

laughing and free through the woods, to be caught and crushed in the embrace of a handsome soldier or forester who looked exactly like Roger. They could have loved without heeding custom or dowries or rank. She turned restlessly, realising the futility of her fantasies.

On an impulse she flung off her soft linen shift and donned her plainest dress and sandals. Her dark woollen cloak she snatched from a wall hook, swirling it round her and pulling up the hood. One last hour of freedom she must have! To run through the trees to a pretended trysting place to meet an imaginary lover, to forget for an hour the torment that lay ahead.

It was an easy task to reach the courtyard, but it required a little lurking in the shadows before she was able to slip past the guard, mingling with the late stragglers and out of the main gate. Crouched in a grassy ditch beyond the bailey wall, she waited for a few moments, her heart pounding with the excitement of what she was doing. Never before had she left the castle alone, always in a closed litter or on horseback with a strong escort of men-at-arms.

She brushed aside her father's horror at her behaviour and ran swiftly to the shadow of the trees. To own the truth, she was a little apprehensive herself, but all fear was swept aside as she raced through the woods, revelling in her freedom.

The night was warm and the breeze fanned her hot cheeks. Alyce flung back the hood of the cloak. Running on and on until she was out of breath, she came at last to a small clearing through which a stream sang softly over the pebbles. Starlight glittered on the water and the murmur of leaves and the sounds of night creatures seemed to touch and enclose this spot with magic. She knelt, peering into the bed of the stream, running her fingers over the smooth pebbles. Her hair fell like silken curtains across her face as she stared at the reflected stars and the shimmering beauty of the moon.

If superstition is true, she told herself, I should see the face of my true love. But only the moon and stars were reflected.

Alyce raised her head and looked across the water. Instinct told her she was not alone, but in this enchanted place she felt no fear. The man stepped from the bushes and she noted his rich clothing, the embroidered tunic, the close-fitting hose and soft leather ankle-boots.

His voice held a touch of amusement as he said, 'Lady of Starlight. Are you real, or will you disappear like a wood nymph if I come close?'

The shadows hid his face as he paused but she caught the glint of a smile.

'Who are you, sir?' Her voice came evenly. Although she felt no fear, her instincts were to keep a distance between them. She was glad he was a gentleman and not some peasant or tavern servant.

'May I not ask the same question of you?'

'I am—my name is—Kate. From the village,' she added hastily, thinking it wiser to conceal her identity. 'And you, sir?'

'Just a restless traveller. I am with a party bound for the castle yonder. Do you know it, Kate-from-the-village?'

Was he laughing at her, guessing she was Alyce? 'I know it. The Lord of Beaumont lives there.'

He took a step forward and faced her across the stream. The moonlight fell fully upon him. His hand, resting on the hilt of his dagger, caught her attention. The heavy signet ring he wore was carved with an emblem she recognised. Her heart jerked. How could she forget the Boveney arms?

'I suppose,' she said carefully, 'that you are come for the wedding?'

He nodded. 'I rode ahead of the main party.'

She knew him now. Even by moonlight there could be no mistake. His face, a little older and fuller but well-remembered, was smooth and unmarked. This must be Gilbert, her groom-to-be.

She regarded him warily, letting her hair drift across her face as she bowed her head slightly. If she could not love him, might she perhaps achieve a measure of contentment? He had kissed her mercilessly in the corridor that night, but that had been done in anger. Before the tournament he had been courteous enough. But what she could not fathom was the report that her father gave of a man determined on matrimony. Why should Sir Gilbert be so determined? He could pick and choose, according to Roger. Her dowry? As an only child it would be a rich one. Was he such an expensive fellow that her charms as a considerable heiress were the main attraction? Or was he tired of being importuned to marry so constantly by his family and she possessed the right attributes?

'You are eager to get to the castle?' she asked, hopeful that he might speak in terms of some affection, however small.

He regarded her frankly. 'Eager? Not in the least. These ceremonies and feasts are too dreary for my taste, but one must obey one's father and simulate enthusiasm. It is a duty, nothing more. I'd rather be with a hunting party any day. Or in your village, my dear, where the girls are pretty and very friendly towards restless travellers.'

She was taken aback by his statement. 'But—but don't you have any curiosity or—or feelings for the Lady Alyce?'

He shrugged. 'A pretty enough wench to pass an idle hour, and the dowry is said to be generous. What more need one know? Tonight my curiosity is for Kate-from-the-village. Why have I not met you there before? I would have remembered so beautiful a maiden.' He laughed. 'Or did we perhaps sport only in the dark?'

There was a hollow feeling in the pit of her stomach. So it was the dowry! She was merely incidental. To possess one was to be forced to take the other. And he had not even remembered her! A few polite words tossed carelessly to the daughter of the house, then her image dismissed as if she was nothing but the vessel required to continue the de Boveney line. How different from Roger who had aroused in her such passion, and to whom she would have joyfully borne a dozen de Boveneys.

He was across the stream in two strides, and he grasped her wrists, drawing her to him. Her eyes flew to his face, the face she remembered as being sardonic and mocking, was now filled with arrogant sensuality. He was smiling, but it was the confident and practised smile of one who had never met rejection.

In that moment she noted the signs of hard living, the lines round the wine-brightened eyes. How he had changed! She had thought him hard, but never self-indulgent. What kindness was there in this man who thought only to gratify his senses? Was this how she would fare in his keeping?

His lips found hers. They were hard but damp, reminding her of the kisses of Count Hubert. She shuddered and struggled wildly as his hand thrust into the neck of her tunic.

'Let me go!' she demanded furiously. 'How dare you?'

He laughed, drawing her closer. 'Not just yet, my girl. One doesn't come across starlit maidens every night. We must make the most of the opportunity. Tomorrow is for duty —tonight for pleasure. And such pleasure I will teach you, my little nymph!'

She was reminded even more forcibly of Count Hubert but this was a true knight and chivalrous, she had imagined, one who would accept a rebuttal with courtesy. But in the face of his obvious determination, her illusion of knightly virtues crumbled like shattered crystal and the pain bit sharply.

'But you will not take your pleasure with me,' she returned, her voice haughty. His eyes narrowed.

'You put on the airs of a lady but you are from the village or you would not be here at this hour. I suppose you have learned grand ideas from your betters at the castle. A chambermaid, perhaps?'

'I am no one's servant, nor am I a village girl.'

'But you said you were, so naturally I must take your word for it. How can I be blamed for treating you as such?'

'I think you are hateful.'

He grinned, still confident. 'I cannot think you will remain long of that opinion, my Lady of Starlight, when you see the gold pieces I carry.' His hand came up and cupped her chin, drawing her face to his. 'I like a wench with spirit. I accept your challenge, girl. Fight as you will, I shall make you mine and taste of your sweetness.' His voice thickened with desire.

A ripple of panic ran through Alyce. She twisted away violently, and her freed hand swung round and struck wildly. The metal bracelet on her wrist caught him on the cheek, its edge scoring deep into the skin.

His face darkened and the lips were no longer smiling but down-turned in fury. He mouthed something savagely and staggered back, loosening his hold. Tearing herself free, she darted into a thicket of trees, panic sending her flying madly, heedless of direction. Faster and faster, stumbling and crashing through the bushes, snatching her cloak free from twigs and brambles she fled. Anywhere, as long as it was far away from Gilbert.

At first she thought she heard pursuing footsteps, but as she twisted and turned they grew fainter. She ran on, unaware of the tears that poured down her cheeks. Fear and disgust mingled with a hatred so deep that she believed she would welcome death rather than be joined in marriage to that man. Even if her father beat her—and he surely would for the escapade itself—she would refuse to do his bidding. Far better a bleak future immured for ever in a convent than one of misery with a lecherous man for husband.

Her whole being revolted at the thought. Of course men took mistresses, but surely there was compliance on both sides? One did not expect a true knight to roam the countryside molesting any woman who strayed into his path. She had thought Sir Gilbert more particular, but this experience had shocked her into a realisation that she had misjudged him badly.

Never—never—would she marry him!

CHAPTER FIFTEEN

THE woods were thinning, the trees getting sparser and Alyce could see the sky without a dense lacework of leaf and branch. Her panic had subsided, leaving her desolate and aching, as if all the dreams she had ever known had been done to death in this one last hour. She hugged her cloak round her, trying to discover where she was. A clearing ahead, with a glimpse of a well-worn track running through it, told her she might be nearer the castle than she thought. Perhaps it was the road from the hills, the one she had looked at so often, hoping to see the white stallion appear. Her breath caught on a sob. If Roger ever came again it would not be to claim her, but to witness her marriage to his brother.

She began to run once more, not really caring if she never did find the castle again. There was nothing of happiness there. But with her habit of duty and obedience, she realised she must return, if only to make a final plea to her father.

Half-blinded by tears, she burst from the woods and found herself surrounded by horses and armed men. They were all about her, as startled as she was. Arms raised, she screamed in terror as the powerful flanks of a shying horse backed into her, then she was gripped and dragged out of the way, her face pressed hard against chainmail with strong arms supporting her.

There was an exclamation from her captor as he held her away from him and looked into her face. Through her tears she saw that he was elderly and grey-haired, with eyes that narrowed as he stared at her.

'Come, little lady, you should not be running through the

woods so late.' His voice was soft and cultured. 'I will take you home.'

'But you don't know who or where——' she began.

'Hush, my dear, I know enough. Trust me.' He lifted her easily on to the saddle and swung up behind, urging the horse forward. His cloak covered her, masking her from the other riders. 'We are headed for the same place. Don't talk yet.'

The party moved on, the horses spreading out, and Alyce thought it safe to speak without being overheard.

'How did you know?' she whispered.

'I recognised you, but do not fear betrayal. Only tell me, were you running away from home?'

'Oh, no, I dare not be so disobedient. I wanted to be alone for a little while before—before tomorrow.'

He nodded. 'Not very wise, my dear, but understandable. Did you have an assignation in the woods? Perhaps with someone to whom you wished to say farewell?'

She raised a shocked countenance. 'No! I swear it.'

His eyes looked into hers keenly. That probing glance seemed somehow familiar. Where had she encountered it before? This man was a complete stranger to her.

'But you were frightened,' he insisted. 'Something happened to you before we met.'

Her chin came up and she stared ahead, saying stonily, 'I was surprised by one I mistook for a true knight.' But her voice trembled as she spoke.

'But you came to no harm? Tell me the truth, lady.' His voice took on a hardness and she cast him a quick look, wondering, then shook her head.

'I—I struck him and ran.'

His mouth tightened, whether in anger or amusement she could not decipher, but he asked no more questions and they journeyed in silence until the castle was reached. In the shadow of the gate he allowed her to slide from the saddle as the sentries challenged the party.

LADY OF STARLIGHT

In the flurry of shouted orders and the noise of opening gates, Alyce flattened herself against the wall, slipping in behind the horses as they swung through. Hooded and cloaked, she drifted as one more shadow, unseen beside a sumpter horse. Away from the torchlight, she circled the bailey wall, moving in the darkness until she was near the side door that led through the herb garden. From there she was able to make her way silently up the stairs while all attention was directed towards the arrivals.

Once in her room she threw off her cloak and lay huddled on the bed, face down, her fingers kneading the soft fur. She had no idea of the time, she only knew she must seek out her father and plead with him to free her from this marriage.

After a time her shivering stopped. Still cold but quite calm now, she removed her torn clothing and washed off the marks and dust of her flight. Then she slipped into her nightgown and dropped a heavily embroidered ankle-length robe over her head. She tidied her hair but left it loose.

The castle was quiet as she moved from her room. The torches, burning in their brackets on the wall, showed only empty passageways. The night was cool and she hugged the thick robe to her shoulders, hoping desperately that her father would be prepared to listen to her.

Her slippers made little sound as she rounded the corner. The moon cast its glow through a small high window, the barred fingers of light repeating themselves on the flagstones. From a seat set in a stone recess, a figure rose suddenly. Alyce stopped dead, a strangled scream rising in her throat.

'Forgive me, my lady, I did not mean to startle you.' The voice was familiar. He stepped forward into the moonlight and she saw the scar running across his cheekbone.

Her first impulse was to throw herself into his arms, but she held back, fighting for self-control. Her body ached with longing to feel again the hard-muscled body so close to hers, the fierce kisses and the tender touch of his hands on her breasts. But he must never know how much he had hurt her by accepting her betrothal to his brother. He had not fought the world to keep her as he had promised. Just words—empty words! Let it count in my favour whatever befalls, he had said. Had he known even then on the battlements that their future was not to be together?

Her regard was cold and his smile faded. But the words came swiftly before she could restrain them.

'How could you do this to me?'

He frowned, his eyes narrowing. 'Is this not what you wanted? They told me you were well-pleased with the betrothal. How was I to think otherwise?'

She stared at him helplessly. How had they convinced him her desire was for Gilbert? A flush mounted to her cheeks as she recalled her almost wanton behaviour on the battlements. She looked down to avoid his penetrating gaze.

'I—I have no wish for this marriage,' she said haltingly. 'I intend to seek my father and beg him to put a stop to it. If only I had known the truth sooner I might have influenced his decision.' She raised her eyes briefly to whisper, 'How could you deceive me so?' then turned swiftly before he should see her tears. 'I must go before it is too late.'

'It is already too late!'

She swung round, dismayed by his sharp tone.

'The royal signature is on the bond and the King gone to Normandy,' he said harshly. 'It would almost be treason to rescind it. I doubt that our fathers would risk the King's displeasure. They are together in the great hall, so you cannot go to your father privately. Their minds are rigidly set on this marriage, and nothing you say will alter things.'

Pain was reflected for an instant on his face, then a mask descended, banishing all expression. So he too was as unhappy as she was. Her eyes closed on the sight of those beloved features. Never must she recall their passion again. It had no place in her future.

He gazed at her for a long moment. 'Do you fear love so much, Alyce?' he asked, his voice roughened by emotion.

'Love?' she choked. 'Is that what it is called? 'Twas more like passion based on lust than on tenderness. If I had not been so foolish——'

Here she stopped, appalled. This was his brother! How could she tell the truth of that outrage in the woods? Her shoulders drooped.

'If it is already too late, I can do nothing then.' She spoke in a toneless voice, blinking quickly as all hope drained from her.

'Neither of us can do anything, Alyce. We were both deceived, it seems, but for the sake of the King we must accept it.' He turned from her.

Her smile was bitter. 'Very well, but it will be little better than the future de Louches planned for me.'

She broke off as he swung round swiftly, his face darkening with anger, his eyes fierce and hostile. 'By the Rood, my lady, you give the de Boveneys scant praise to liken us to that one. How dare you show such ingratitude?'

Pressing a hand to her aching head she stammered, 'Forgive me, sir, I did not mean to insult your house. I am truly grateful for that rescue, but I am afraid—desperately afraid. Help me—I beg of you.'

His arms rose as if to clasp her to him. She shrank away, unable to accept that little comfort without humiliating herself by pleading for his love.

The arms dropped. He turned to the wall, leaning his forehead on his raised arm. 'Go to bed, Alyce,' he said in a strained voice. 'There is nothing I can do.'

It seemed only minutes before Meg was shaking her shoulder. 'Come, my lady. The girls have brought hot water and we must make you beautiful for your groom.' Her tone was deliberately cheerful, but a glance at the pale face showed her that no change of heart had taken place. 'Drink this milk,' she coaxed, 'while it is still hot.'

Alyce climbed wearily from her bed. 'I don't want to get married,' she muttered. 'I hate him.'

'Don't speak so, my lady, please. He is handsome and well-mannered. I don't doubt many girls would be eager to take your place.'

They would be welcome to it, Alyce reflected bitterly. She stood in silence as they dressed her. First the short white linen chemise, then the sleeveless undergown. Over this went a long embroidered tunic, and finally a girdle of gold, knotted and tasselled. Her hair was parted in the middle, plaited and bound with gold braid before the veil was set in place. She was glad of the veil. No one, not even Meg, should see the bleak despair in her eyes.

Her mind flinched from all thought of the man she was pledged to marry. How foolish of her to dream of love and tenderness! Those things were for people like Meg.

Her ladies escorted her to the chapel entrance where her father waited. She passed Ranulf and Wilfred. Both bowed and she responded with a stiff smile, then looked without interest at the tall stranger beside Earl Robert. He turned and she caught her breath. He was her rescuer of the previous night!

'My lord of Boveney, daughter,' said her father, and Alyce sank trembling into a curtsy. De Boveney raised her, smiling into her face, his fingers pressing hers encouragingly.

'Don't look so fearful, my child. Gilbert will make you a fine husband. You have nothing to fear, for he loves you truly and in all honour.'

She raised her eyes, her thoughts bitter. Even now, after our meeting last night, you tell me that? But then, she realised, he didn't know and she had not spoken the name of the man in the woods.

'He is, at times, too preoccupied with royal affairs, but I don't doubt he will find more joy in your company than the King's.'

'Yes, my lord,' she replied in a hollow voice, repressing a shudder. How little he knew of his son's affairs. Royal, indeed!

'But not always with the King's knowledge, I understand, from what you told me last night,' put in her father, his eyes twinkling. 'Not above a little deception of the King at times, the young cub!' He shook his head admiringly. 'He kept up the masquerade even as they all rode off with the King, and not one of us suspected it that day.'

De Boveney laughed. 'Not even I when they returned home, as close as I am to them both.'

Earl Robert glanced down into Alyce's puzzled face. 'You remember the tournament, Alyce?'

The tournament? 'Yes, I remember.' As if it was yesterday, she said to herself. Roger so brave and gallant, taking on an opponent of Sir Lionel's stature. She blinked quickly. 'The day Roger was unhorsed and—and hurt?'

Her eyes widened in amazement as the two men roared with laughter.

'That's what we all thought,' said Earl Robert. 'Until they got him to the marquee and took off his armour to dress his wound. But it was not Roger at all. It was Gilbert, as my lord revealed to me last night.'

'But why?' stammered Alyce. 'I—I don't understand. I thought it was Roger who issued the challenge.'

De Boveney's voice held a hint of dryness. 'So it was, but the contests were lasting too long for him and he had an assignation he preferred to keep, so Gilbert took his place. When he regained consciousness, he begged the squires not to announce the deception to the King in case Roger was called coward.'

'And we all assumed the bandaged knight was Roger,'

added Earl Robert, 'for they changed horses to carry on the deception when they left.'

Alyce spoke slowly, trying to still the turmoil in her mind. She had to be sure. 'So Gilbert bears the scar—not Roger?'

'That's right. Thank heavens it was no worse, or you'd be short of a bridegroom today, my lady, and such a one whose heart is given but once. Believe me, Alyce, for I know my sons too well.'

A bubble of happiness began to rise in Alyce. The man in the woods had been Roger. A changed and dissipated creature, so different from her long-held image of him. And last night in the corridor—she caught her breath—that had been Gilbert, her bridegroom-to-be!

And she had let him think this marriage abhorrent to her! He must have thought she knew the truth of the masquerade and was rejecting him while she, still deceived, had succeeded in convincing him of her distaste.

'Although,' de Boveney went on thoughtfully, 'as to scars, Roger bids fair to join him, for he has a cut cheekbone this morning. Walked into a hawthorn bush last night on his way back from the village. I sent him home.'

Their eyes met, both remembering. De Boveney smiled. 'I would say that Gilbert's scar was earned more honourably. Wouldn't you, my lady?'

Alyce nodded speechlessly, her amber eyes grown luminous in a face that glowed with an ethereal radiance.

'Are you ready, daughter?' asked Earl Robert, extending his arm for her to take. Her eyes met Lord de Boveney's in silent appeal. That penetrating look she had thought so familiar last night was there, and with it a complete understanding.

'Let the priest wait another five minutes, Robert,' he suggested. 'My lady needs a moment to compose herself. Indulge her, old friend, for this is a special time in the life of any young maid.' Before Earl Robert could speak, he went on, 'A few turns in a quiet place adds serenity to the mind. I always think a garden—in particular a sweet-scented one—the ideal place.'

Earl Robert gazed from one face to the other. Some instinct warned him to hold his tongue and agree to the short delay, so he smiled and nodded. 'Very well. But five minutes only, or the priest will be upon us demanding to know why we keep such eminence waiting.'

Alyce murmured something incoherently and fled to the herb garden, her heart thudding like a blacksmith's hammer, in joy but also in trepidation. How to convince him she had no idea at the moment, but the truth must be told before the ceremony took place.

Pushing aside her veil, she entered the herb garden slowly. She saw him immediately and stopped. His back was towards her. He was moodily kicking at the earth that bordered the small lawn. Her heart jerked as she surveyed the tall, lithe figure, the close-fit tunic that showed the width of his shoulders before tapering to the slim waist and to the strong, well-shaped legs.

'Sir Gilbert,' she called softly.

The glance he threw over his shoulder was not encouraging, and he returned to contemplating the hole he had dug with the toe of his soft leather jewelled boot.

Alyce moved forward, knowing that the initiative must be hers alone. She stopped within a few feet of him and gazed down at the soil-covered boot.

'You are ruining your wedding boots, sir,' she observed mildly, then was struck by the utter banality of her remark. Her gaze rose as he turned to face her fully and fold his arms. His look was cold.

'So?'

'I—I would prefer my bridegroom to be elegant in all things.'

'An elegant statue, Alyce, where passion—or lust as you term it—has no place?'

Alyce took a deep painful breath. She could expect no help from this cold stranger. The time for honesty was at hand.

'My love, body and soul, was given to the man who killed Count Hubert. To him only will I respond with the passion he aroused in me. That man I will love and honour to my dying day. Whatever his name, I will cleave to no other.'

'And which man is that?'

'A man who carried a scar upon his cheek, a scar I believed to have been earned at the tournament.'

'And yet you shrank in horror from that scarred man last night.'

She smiled. 'Last night I was unaware of the truth. I turned from him for fear of showing my love too brazenly when I was pledged, as I thought, to marry another. I only learned of the deception a few moments ago, from my lord of Boveney. The man I loved denied it not when I called him Roger. Perhaps you can explain that to me, for I can think of no reason.'

'I had only one reason, my lady, for such deception. You came into my arms on the battlements as naturally as a woman gives herself to her lover. My heart has been yours since that day of the tournament, yet your dreams were still of Roger. You were a child then and full of illusions, but in my arms you were a woman—my woman!

'I wanted you so badly I let you think me Roger. I dared not risk owning the truth until I had you secured by the King's bond.' He held himself stiffly, his face still impassive. 'It was not knightly conduct, I admit. I must only earn your scorn by such a trick.'

'Not scorn, Sir Gilbert, but gratitude.' She laughed a little shakily. 'You will never know how much. My illusions were dispelled for ever last night.'

'In the woods?' he asked.

'How—how did you know that?'

'My father mentioned finding you alone and in some distress. I knew that Roger was out seeking diversion—it has become a way of life with him. You could not have been happy there, Alyce.'

'I realised that when he didn't even recognise me. But I took him for you, and was appalled to think I was betrothed to such a one.' She frowned in thought. 'Why did you let me think he was the victor in the bear hunt—which seems now to have been the start of all this deception?'

'You took it for granted he was, so I kept silent, hoping it might serve to keep him by your side and away from the village girls.'

Alyce glanced over her shoulder. 'We have been allowed only five minutes alone, Sir Gilbert. That time must surely be over. They will be sending Ranulf any moment now.'

Turning back to him, she encountered the look he had worn on the battlements, his brown eyes alive and demanding.

'Then we must not waste these last few seconds with words, my heart.'

His arms drew her gently towards him but the lips that descended on hers were fierce. Alyce felt herself melt into his embrace and she clung to him with a passion that equalled his own. Her eyes were blinded by the brilliance of the sun and her spirits rose and soared with the trilling birds.

As if a thousand candles had been lit in her heart, her body flamed with a desire that could never be quenched, though she live a lifetime of love with this man. To him she would hold fast, as Matilda had held to William, and glory in being possessed by this truest of the King's knights.

Masquerade
Historical Romances

Intrigue excitement romance

Don't miss
February's
other enthralling Historical Romance title

CAMILLA
by Sara Orwig

Camilla Hyde's only hope of escaping back to England from the ruins of Washington in that fateful year of 1814 lies not with the invading British soldiers but with Jared Kingston, a surly English nobleman turned planter, who reluctantly rescues her from the ravages of war. With this total stranger, Camilla treks across the huge American continent to Louisiana enduring unimaginable hardships. She is willing to travel with the Devil himself if it means she can get home to her beloved England.

Hardly have they reached the South when the Battle of New Orleans commences and, once more, Camilla is thrown into the thick of battle. And it is to Jared that once more she is forced to turn for help ...

You can obtain this title today from your local paperback retailer